"Stan Dotson's writing embodies compassion for the needs of others, awe at the beauty of existence, and the capacity to take suffering seriously without falling into despair. This book walks with a handful of people on paths many of us have never seen, beginning eighty thousand years ago and arriving in the present moment. I'm so grateful *Where Are They Going?* is here. Stan is not only a trustworthy guide, but a brilliant writer who is touched by that rare thing: how to take life seriously and how to show us the way."

—GARETH HIGGINS, AUTHOR OF *HOW NOT TO BE AFRAID*, CO-FOUNDER OF THE PORCH COMMUNITY OF TRANSFORMATIVE STORYTELLING

"Stan Dotson uses the word 'magic' more than once in *Where Are They Going?* to describe phenomenal encounters and occurrences. The term can be applied to the creative work he has accomplished in this beautiful book. With ancestral history as warp and current Cuban reality as weft, he has woven a unique and compelling lyrical tapestry. Dotson writes of being 'captivated' by Cuba's people and culture, and through his eyes and heart, we too are drawn into the magic."

—JOYCE HOLLYDAY, AUTHOR OF *PILLAR OF FIRE*

"Stan Dotson, thank you for sharing your insight into the cultural threads that make up the exquisite tapestry of the Cuban people—with particular attention given to those who have responded to the call to stay in the land they love! These stories, imaginatively interwoven with history, literature, music and spirituality, demonstrate what it truly means to be a friend of the Cuban people. Thank you for these deeper glimpses into the soul of Cuba!"

—PAULA CLAYTON DEMPSEY, BAPTIST MINISTER, FREQUENT PILGRIM TO CUBA

"To say that Stan Dotson's book provides compelling bio sketches of five current, unsung Cuban citizens is like saying Hemingway wrote about whales and bells and loved Cuban rum. I don't know what to call this genre, but it includes epochal allegory, the sweep of a towering historical novel, combined with the illumination reminiscent of the best of Terry Gross' interviews. Dotson offers resplendent stories, served up with the flair of a virtuoso storyteller."

—KEN SEHESTED, AUTHOR OF *IN THE LAND OF THE WILLING: LITANIES, PRAYERS, POEMS, AND BENEDICTIONS*

Where Are They Going?

For Wayne –
Gracias for being such a
faithful companion on the journey!

Where Are They Going?

Stories and Backstories of Five Cubans

Blessings

STAN DOTSON

RESOURCE *Publications* · Eugene, Oregon

WHERE ARE THEY GOING?
Stories and Backstories of Five Cubans

Resource Publications
An Imprint of Wipf and Stock Publishers
199 W. 8th Ave., Suite 3
Eugene, OR 97401

www.wipfandstock.com

PAPERBACK ISBN: 978-1-6667-6685-1
HARDCOVER ISBN: 978-1-6667-6686-8
EBOOK ISBN: 978-1-6667-6687-5

03/02/23

All lyrics from Silvio Rodríguez songs are used here with his permission.

To Luis Pérez Martinto
vaya con Dios

¿A dónde van ahora mismo estos cuerpos,
que no puedo nunca dejar de alumbrar?
¿Acaso nunca vuelven a ser algo?
¿Acaso se van? ¿Y a dónde van?
¿A dónde van?[1]

Where are these bodies going right now,
that I can never stop illuminating?
Will they never be something again?
Are they leaving? And where are they going?
Where are they going?

1. Rodríguez, Silvio, "*¿A Dónde Van?*" *Mujeres*. Fonomusic, 1978. Album.

Contents

Acknowledgments

I am indebted to all the friends and family members who read various drafts of the book and offered helpful feedback. Special thanks to Dale Roberts and Beth Honeycutt for their insightful suggestions, and to Kim Christman, my life-partner and collaborator in this Cuba adventure, for her constant support and encouragement.

I am also grateful for Melania Melero Couarraze and Luis Pérez Martinto, who painstakingly went through the book with me, paragraph by paragraph, checking the accuracy of the *cubanía*[2] as well as helping me translate it into Spanish.

Special thanks to Silvio Rodríguez, Cuba's most prolific singer-song-writer, for his generous words of support, and for granting permission to use his lyrics for the book title and for framing each chapter. *¿A Dónde Van? (Where Are They Going?)* was the song that first hooked me on his expansive catalog of music.

Before discovering Silvio, my knowledge of Cuban music was limited to the old trova made famous in Ry Cooder's classic documentary, "Buena Vista Social Club." It took me several more years to discover *nueva trova*, the music of the new troubadours who emerged in the post-Revolution 1960s. Silvio Rodriguez, one of the founders of *nueva trova*, is among the most beloved of this generation of singer-songwriters.

My exposure to Silvio came through a trio of young Cuban musicians, Yivi and Dianelys and Lisbeth, who have come to be like daughters for Kim and me. I am deeply grateful to them for teaching me to appreciate the genius of Silvio. Part of his allure lies in the theme of this book; his life is a series of comings and goings. Silvio is a world traveler, but he always comes home, and he always gives voice to the people of his homeland. Each of the chapters here begins with lyrics from one of his songs, in an attempt to honor that commitment to stay rooted in the *patria*.

2. *Cubanía* is a word used to describe the essence of being Cuban and the qualities that comprise Cuban culture.

Finally, I give thanks to the protagonists of the book, whose stories demonstrate the breadth and depth of what it means to be Cuban: Sila Reyna Cervantes, Orestes Roca Santana, Alexis Morales O'Farrill, Lázaro Ceballos Fernández, and Luis Pérez Martinto.

Preface

Let's Walk

Vamos a andar con todas las banderas trenzadas de manera que no haya soledad. . .Vamos a andar para llegar a la vida.[3]
—SILVIO RODRIGUEZ, VAMOS A ANDAR

Colón, Cuba
Friday, March 4, 2022 CE
9:30 a.m.

"*Everybody's* going to the United States!" Nestor, our driver, was on a rant, giving a running commentary on the day's news to a van-load of musicians who were embarking on a four-province tour.[4] "After all," he continued, "the US is a nation of immigrants! But *nobody* wants to emigrate to Cuba—" His commentary came to a sudden halt. Then, with a nod and grin in our direction, he added a side-comment, "except for Stan and Kim."

Nestor's "everybody" is hyperbole, an exaggeration I've heard for years. The stereotypical picture of Cubans longing to escape and seek their fortunes in the land of the free is a prevailing narrative, especially in US

3. Translated: "Let's walk with all the flags braided in a such a way that there will be no loneliness. . . Let's walk to arrive at life." Rodríguez, Silvio, "Vamos a Andar." *Rabo de Nube.* Areito, 1979. Album.

4. The musical group of which Kim and I are a part, "Con Fe Mezcla'o" (With Mixed Faith), blends together the music of the Beatles and Silvio Rodríguez, along with songs of faith, all inspired by the same muse.

circles. I even had a State Department diplomat once tell me that she, like all embassy personnel, had been trained to make the assumption that every Cuban would jump at any chance to migrate north. It did not alter her stereotype when I told her that over the past thirty years my wife Kim and I have hosted or helped host upwards of thirty Cuban visitors, some multiple times, and all but four returned to Cuba, despite great pressure from family and friends in Miami to stay.

As we rode along Cuba's central highway, with Nestor dodging pothole after pothole like a slalom skier maneuvering around the gates, we could see reality contradicting the exaggerated claim. Through every little town we passed, like Colón, named for the famed explorer, we saw people going places, but the US was not their destination. Some were going to school; others were going to work. Some were going in search of their daily bread; others were going to a health clinic or hospital. Some were going to the theater, others to a concert.

Contrary to another stereotype, few of them were going in a classic car. Outside of the tourist sector, you don't see that many automobiles in Cuba, and of the ones that are on the road, there are more '70s-era Russian Ladas than there are '57 Chevys. Other forms of coming and going in Cuba include old buses, motor scooters, and bicycles with multi-patched tires, but by far the most prevalent means of getting from one place to another is by foot. People walk a lot in Cuba. That is probably why one of the most commonly heard greetings in Cuba is: *¿Cómo andamos?* Literally, "How are we walking?"

In fairness to Nestor, while millions do continue making their daily walk on Cuban soil, there is a relatively large number of immigrants giving credence to his rant. Thousands of Cubans are walking out these days, bolting, much as they did back in the 1990s when Cuba endured its decade-long "Special Period" of economic hardship after the fall of the Soviet Union. Now, the tightening of US sanctions, coupled with COVID's two-year closure of the tourist industry, and the country's own untimely economic reforms, have all conspired to plummet Cuba into another Special Period, some say worse than that of the 90s. It should come as no surprise that traumatized people are once again fleeing.

This time around, though, the exodus is not in homemade rafts, but in caravans. The pilgrims' journey starts with a flight to Nicaragua (which does not require a visa for Cubans to enter), and from there "coyotes" (aka traffickers) will carry them on the long trek through Honduras and Guatemala into Mexico. There is danger at every step, especially on this crossing into Mexico, where they have to deal with bands of outlaws and corrupt police, all of whom are glad to receive bribes from the travelers who then make their way north to the Rio Grande, where they will take their chances with the river and border patrol.

While the plight of these immigrants is daily fare on the news, it really isn't "news." People living in contexts of scarcity have always migrated toward contexts of surplus. The Bible would be missing its own Exodus story had Jacob not sent his sons from famine-stricken Canaan down to Egypt to access the empire's seven-year surplus of grain.

It doesn't matter whether or not you have done your homework as to the reasons why Pharaoh's belly was full while Jacob's stomach was growling, why an imperial power prospers while a marginalized country suffers. Nor does it matter if you know good and well that prospering empires generally gain their abundance through predatory practices that impoverish their neighbors. What matters is satiating your hunger pangs, gaining access to shelves that never lack for an abundance of meats, cheeses, beers, breads, you name it.

I personally know more than a few Cuban immigrants who have chosen to seek out those over-stocked shelves in one of the fifty states in our nation of immigrants. They are well on their way to becoming "American,"[5] adding their *cubanía* to the diverse cultural mix. But it is not entirely true that my ranting friend's hyperbolic "everybody" is joining the huddled masses at the US border. I also know many Cubans who have flown the coop and landed in other countries around the world. Some are well on their way to becoming Canadian, others Brazilian, French, Spanish, Dutch or Russian.

There was more than a kernel of truth in Nestor's side-comment about me and Kim, though; we *are* traveling against the coyote-led traffic, hoping to fly our comfortable coop and land in the more challenging confines of Cuba. As thousands flee the island, here we are, trying to figure out some way to get back to Matanzas, our home base there, hopefully to stay. According to the Cuban constitution, there are only two official routes in the journey to permanent residency for people not born on the island: one, if the President of the country extends a special invitation, and two, if you marry a Cuban. We jokingly mentioned to a couple in Matanzas that maybe we could get a divorce and find two Cubans to marry; they responded with great enthusiasm and volunteered to file their own divorce papers and become our surrogate spouses. As tempting as that was, we are instead trying to figure out how many degrees of separation exist between us and President Miguel Diaz-Canel.

5. While the term "American" is commonly misused as a synonym for citizens of the United States, it properly refers to citizens of any country in the three "Americas"—North, Central, and South, as well as the Caribbean islands.

But this book is not about us and our journey to Cuba, (although you can read a bit of that in the epilogue). The heart of *Where Are They Going?* narrates what we have found there, or better, *who* we have found there. It is the story of five Cubans who, despite many opportunities to do otherwise, have decided to stay, to continue their daily walk on Cuban soil. When people ask me why it is I would want to live in Cuba, I have found no better way to answer than to tell stories of our Cuban friends. They are what attract me. Their spirit, their creativity, their resilience, their ingenuity, their faith; it all creates a strong gravitational pull.

The stories of these five friends are not isolated; they represent the experiences of millions of others who are determined to remain Cuban, to remain in Cuba, despite the constant pressures of an economy in collapse, and despite the incessant pounding of propaganda enticing them to greener pastures. One friend assured me that he would be there to turn out the lights, were he to be the last surviving Cuban living in Cuba.

I have no reason to judge or question those who have decided to carry their *cubanía* with them to other lands. But this book sets out to tell a different set of stories, stories not readily heard in US media outlets. We get virtually all of our news about Cuba filtered through the narrow lens of those who have left, whose feet now trod different soil. A few stories from those who remain and continue putting one foot in front of the other there on the island might give us a wider lens through which to see and understand Cuba and the Cubans' walk of life.

I can imagine that every Cuban is more than familiar with the tension voiced in the famous punk-rock question of the Clash—"Should I stay or should I go?" While the five protagonists in this book have answered the question with a firm decision to stay, they carry with them the long history of ancestors from around the globe who answered differently. Each of them has a counterpart in their lineage who left Old World homelands to begin a walk and embark on journeys that would eventually land them on Cuban shores. Some of those giant-step journeys were taken for adventure, some in search of treasure, some to escape scarcity, some by cruel force.

This book will not only tell the stories of twenty-first century Cubans—Sila and Orestes and Alexis and Lázaro and Luis—it will also tell the stories of their counterparts from centuries ago, the ancestors whose physical and cultural DNA spirals through their cells. It will be story and backstory—biography and historical fiction, woven together. My hope, perhaps my fantasy, in writing this is that some reader out there will be as captivated as I am by these stories, will feel the same attraction to and love for these people, so that we will not be the only ones in the US trying to find a way to emigrate to Cuba.

Prologue

First Steps

En busca de un sueño, Dios vino a la tierra . . .
En busca de un sueño, van generaciones.[1]

—SILVIO RODRÍGUEZ, EN BUSCA DE UN SUEÑO

Go back far enough, and you might be able to trace the very first step of the long march that led to the existence of a people group known as "Cubans" to some of the earth's earliest humans. One fine day some eighty millennia ago, while tilling their African garden of Eden, these initial pilgrims felt some powerful push or pull that propelled them away from their Cross River[2] wetland paradise, and set them off on a journey toward other lands.

These exiles from paradise eventually filled the earth with people who came to self-identify as Guanahatabey or Spanish or Dutch or French. The steps toward becoming Cuban involved people claiming these identities, along with many others, feeling yet another push or pull that would prompt them to leave one established home and journey toward another. For the Africans who had not joined that initial exodus from Eden eighty thousand years ago, the steps toward becoming "Afro-Cuban" was all push

1. Translated: "In search of a dream, God came to earth. . . In search of a dream, generations venture out." Rodríguez, Silvio. "En busca de un sueño." *Descartes.* Fono-music, 1998. Album.

2. While some scientists pinpoint the Zambezi wetland of northern Botswana as the "cradle" of our human species, others prefer a "multi-regional" African model that has humanity emerging from various "Edens" across the African continent. With this theory, the Cross River Delta would have served as one of those paradise points.

and no pull, as they were forcibly captured and squeezed into the belly of slave ships.

One thing is certain, then, about Sila and Orestes and Alexis and Lázaro and Luis (the people you will get to know in this book): they are like all Cubans in this respect; their forefathers and foremothers all came from somewhere. And the people who had lived in that "somewhere," perhaps for generations, perhaps for millennia, they, too, had ancestors who had arrived from somewhere else. And like their ancestors, these five have had to learn how to manage the tension of opposing centrifugal and centripetal forces, the competing impulses to stay put and to sail away.

How did this tension, seemingly universal in the human spirit, ever come to be in the first place? Ask a Cuban a question like that, and you might hear a story similar to what follows here in the prologue. Perhaps by engaging our imagination and tracing these opposing drives back to the proverbial beginning, we will have a backdrop for understanding the way the five Cubans of *Where Are They Going?* navigate the tension. Their present-day stories and the backstories that got them here might help us understand a bit better our own internal tug of war.

Cross River Delta, Nigeria
Wednesday, March 20, 80,000 BCE
6:30 a.m.

Imagine being a cutting-edge neuroscientist living and working in the year 80,000 BCE (made possible by travel through a wormhole discovered in a cave system located far beneath your town's nuclear power plant). Your lab is located in the Cross River region of what is now identified on the world map as Nigeria. You arrive at work every day to engage in stunningly euphoric research, investigating and mapping the most significant mutations ever to occur in the homo sapiens brain. To say that these mind-boggling changes will alter the course of world history is a gross understatement. Your research is demonstrating how the fatty-acid-rich cuisine from a fish-based diet is fueling new synapses that are forming in the fledgling human brain, in support of the natural selection process.

Among the new neurons firing are those in the left hemisphere frontal lobe that are beginning to foster the onset of speech, as well as those in the almond-shaped amygdala that are arousing sets of new sensations— discontent and adventure, or to put it another way, boredom with what is, coupled with curiosity for what might be—a tension that is creating the unprecedented impulse to leave the beloved home on the range and explore new horizons.

Later on, you will travel back and publish your findings in prestigious juried journals, and your twenty-first century colleagues will applaud you, concurring with your conclusion that it was this process of genetic mutation, and not climate change pressures, which prompted the sapiens in all their wisdom to leave the long familiar surroundings of the African plains for a protracted march that would eventually populate the globe. The earth scientists and anthropologists were not completely wrong, though; drought and ice were indeed motivating factors along the way for later generations, pressing humankind to continue marching onward and outward.

But these pressures were not responsible for that initial pioneering pilgrimage away from paradise. As you famously said (in the quote you are most associated with), "the genesis was in the genes." Perhaps, and you can leave this up to your fellow researchers down the hall in the behavioral sciences, the new mutations that were occurring eighty thousand years ago were also responsible for the onset of conflict, the first culture clash, as young humanity struggled to answer a completely novel question: "Should I stay or should I go?"

Given the scarcity of neuroscientists in 80,000 BCE Africa, the task of making sense of the changing human dynamics would have fallen instead to the story-tellers, and they would have been spinning a different yarn. With an economy of words (language had not been long in the making), these meaning-makers began crafting tales of the first peoples. They brought to life the first couple, Aganju, whose name means "Tierra Firma" and Yeyé Omo Eja, whose name means "Mother Whose Children are the Fish." This primeval pair shared an innate wisdom about the earth and its abundance of plants, animals, and minerals, how everything works together to hold life in perfect balance.

It was more than wisdom, though; it was faith. As practicing animists[3], Aganju and Yeyé operated on the belief that every single thing in the world was animated by the Life Spirit. All they needed to do to maintain balance was to allow their own Spirit to communicate with the Spirit of whatever they encountered—be it a mango or a mussel or a mushroom—and the Spirit of that object would let them know whether or not it would be wise to serve it up as a side dish for the succulent red snapper or pink salmon caught that day in the Cross River. Some Spirits, such as that of one particular psilocybin mushroom abundant in the surrounding forest, made it clear

The first couple.

---

3. Animism, among humanity's earliest forms of religious faith, involves the belief that everything—plants, animals, inanimate objects, natural phenomena—are imbued with a soul, or a spirit.

that its consumption was taboo. Even one bite would come at great cost to the central nervous system, generating horrific hallucinations that would haunt one's sleep for many moons.

Early one morning, just as the sun was peeping out over the horizon, Shango, the serpentine Fire Spirit, sent bolts of lightning that danced through Aganju and Yeyé and ignited something inside their heads. The crackling and hissing of Shango's flame had a clear message; it granted the couple permission to partake of the prohibited wild mushroom. Aganju and Yeyé listened, and with fear and trembling did what they had never before had the slightest temptation to do. They took a bite. Visions both fascinating and terrifying quickly followed. For hours, or perhaps days, they were bombarded by images and waves of sound they did not and could not understand, because it was a vision of a future far removed. The scenes they witnessed foretold the full range of activity that awaited the story of their descendants, a future filled with infinite possibilities. They saw it all, and suddenly had knowledge of good and evil, complete with the massive potential of each.

The story-tellers would not have had the vocabulary to describe these sights and sounds that swept through Aganju's and Yeyé's minds as they saw the world of their own species' future flash before them—heavenly chamber music and hideous gas chambers, breath-taking machines soaring through the air and breath-stealing machine guns massacring school children, the magnificence of the Sistine Chapel and the monstrosity of priestly pedophilia. Aganju and Yeyé spent weeks, months, maybe even years in a maddening attempt to make sense of it all and discern what to do next. The dilemma was stark—stay put and avoid the possibilities of Auschwitz and Hiroshima, or follow the siren sounds of Beethoven's Ninth and Lecuona's Comparsa? *Should we stay or should we go?*

In the end, the ineffable beauty of the music proved to be a mystery too powerful to resist. So the Spirit of the Camino, Elegguá, the One who opens and closes paths, came to show Aganju and Yeyé the way out of paradise, and then closed the door behind them. They left the glory of their garden with a naked shame of what they were getting ready to make possible, and with a primal scream rising in their now emigrant throats: *A-ah-ahh-ah, ah-ah-ahh-ah.*[4]

---

4. To imagine what this scream might have sounded like, listen to the opening measures of Led Zeppelin's haunting "Immigrant Song."

Chapter 1

Walking with Sila and Her Indigenous Ancestors

Anda, corre donde debas ir.
Anda, que te espera el porvenir.[1]

—Silvio Rodríguez, Requiem

> Matanzas, Cuba
> Sunday, March 29, 2020 CE
> 6:30 p.m.

Sila Reyna Cervantes and her family live in La Vallita, a village small enough to miss if you blink when traveling along the *carretera central* in the Camagüey province, about a nine-hour ride from Matanzas. This "central highway" is something of a misnomer, being as it is for much of the passage from Havana to the eastern end of the island a pot-hole-filled two-lane road. We were with a group of US visitors traveling to La Vallita in a van not too long ago. One of the group was wearing his exercise-monitoring watch, and the bumps along the road led the device to report he had walked two and a half miles while seated in the van.

---

1. Translated: "Go, run where you need to go. Go, the future awaits you." Rodríguez, Silvio. "Requiem." *Causas y Azares*. EGREM, 1986. Album.

Once you get to La Vallita, if there has been a recent rain, your van or car will have to park beside the highway and you will walk the rest of the way, ten minutes or so on a muddy road (your watch would probably count about five hundred steps), to get to Sila's home. You will recognize it as the one with the hand-pumped well in front, and a "President of the CDR"[2] sign on the front door.

We got a phone call from Sila this evening. I love it when she calls; her enthusiastic manner of greeting can lift me up out of the deepest abyss. Her call was timely, as a week of being cooped up in coronavirus quarantine with only the occasional quick jaunt to the park to catch a wifi signal and buy the daily bread and veggies had me in something of a funk. I can picture her broad smile when I answer the phone and she responds—¡Hermanito mío! ¿Cómo tú estás, mi vida? "My little brother! How are you, my life?"

She proceeds to ask about the family in North Carolina, expressing her concern for Juana (Jean, Kim's mom), for Geraldo and Sandra, David and Sisero (my brothers and sisters-in-law), and her friends at the Ecclesia church (her partner church in Asheville, N.C.). They are all family to her. She wants to make sure they are ok and are taking good care in the midst of the growing pandemic. She also asks about her Matanzas family, Orestes and Wanda, Lázaro and Tamara and all the kids. I give a full report on her far-flung spiritual kin, and return the question to her—"How is the family there? Cheo? Anabel and the girls? Amaury and his crew?" We catch up, promise each other prayers, and look forward to getting through the crisis so we can travel again and see each other face to face.

Being face to face with Sila gives you a glimpse into her family heritage. While it is true that the European invasion of Cuba resulted in a virtual genocide of the indigenous population, with nothing like the Cherokee Nation or other reservation communities here, there are people whose facial features demonstrate some degree of kinship with the eradicated peoples. Sila is one of them; she does not need to spit in a tube and send it off to 23andMe to find out she has indigenous blood coursing through her veins. Her's is a copper-toned face with subtle hints of those northeast Asian cheekbones and eyes that developed over the millennia before humans finally started making their way south and arrived at Americus Vespucci's namesake continents.

Sila is a strong woman, a powerful and highly respected force for good in her community. I suspect there is something in the DNA of her character, as well as in her skin tone and facial features, that would reveal an inheritance

2. CDR = Committees for the Defense of the Revolution, set up in the early sixties as a neighborhood watch program to monitor anti-Revolution activities, and it continues to be part of the fabric of Cuban society.

from some of the fierce and forceful women who crossed the grass-covered Bering bridge and turned south so many generations removed.

❖ ❖ ❖

Ural Mountains
Tuesday, March 31, 7,000 BCE   — *A little early to be using March as the name of a month?*
10:10 a.m.

She goes by "Selah." In the old tongue, her name meant "the last word," or "so be it" (in a later tongue, "let it be"). A formidable woman, Selah is proud of her name, never passing up an opportunity to remind the men in her life that she will have the last word. This morning had been no exception. The tribal elders (making decisions for a community of roughly 1000 people) had been debating for days whether to stay and survive another series of moons in the harsh terrain, or to pull up stakes and be on the march again, as their forebears had done so many times before. *Should we stay or should we go?*

Selah's people traced their roots to one Hábel, a progenitor short in stature but long in ability, as his name might suggest to modern readers. That would be a misnomer, though, a false cognate, as the name actually derives from an ancient semitic word meaning "transient." According to the legends, Hábel sired his offspring via a tempestuous relationship with the wind goddess, Oyá, (later to be called *Ruach*). Hence, Hábel and his progeny were the people known to "go with the wind." The moniker fit, for the Habelitos (still diminutive in stature) were a tribe of nomadic hunters and shepherds who went wherever the winds blew the wild game as well as the not-so-wild herds of sheep and goats. Oyá's breezes kept the transients on the move from one tip of the crescent-shaped forest and grasslands to the other and back again. Their fortunes and destiny changed when the winds started blowing them along a seemingly endless, zig-zagging journey north and east a full millennia before Selah's time. They were escaping something strange and horrific that was starting to emerge in the fertile fields of the Jordan River Valley.

Selah's ancestral cousins (on Hábel's brother Chen's side) had long been known as the gathering clan. The name "Chen" (pronounced *chān*) meant "possess" in the semitic tongue, and as the Habelitos would eventually learn, the name betrayed a fundamental character flaw. The Chenites had gained fame for their expertise in finding edible fruits and vegetables and grains along the hunting routes, but after what must have been tens of thousands of years of mutually beneficial collaboration between hunting

Hábel and gathering Chen, the gatherers had come to act like their god-given vocation gave them control and possession over their pickings. The Chen folk also began to complain about the long journeys. They wanted to stay put, to establish themselves in one place and try their hand at taming the wild soil, with a strange notion that in so doing they could store up what they called "produce" (a newly invented word). They forged tools to prune and plow, and claimed that these clumsy contrivances would give them the ability to manipulate the production of what the gods had always provided.

It wasn't long before the Chenites began to resent the way the free-ranging sheep and goats and deer grazed and trod on their new land management projects (here was another new concept: the good earth had been converted into something Chen people called *land*). The four-legged creatures did not understand "land" or "production" any more than did Habelito hunters and herders. When the Chenite complaints and newfound desires fell on deaf ears, they did another new thing—they began turning their pruning hooks into spears and their plowshares into swords, and started attacking brother Hábel and his people (another new word came into the old tongue—*murder*).

What were the Habelitos to do, given their complete ignorance of anything having to do with warfare and violence? Should they stay and wait for the gods to bring justice and restore sanity to their cousins, or should they go in search of greener, uncultivated pastures? The tribe was split. Some of Selah's ancestors did stay and eked out a marginalized survival in the Fertile Crescent. Roving bands of shepherds, they were pushed farther and farther to the edges of what would first become a surplus production center, then a city, then a state, then an empire (or rather a series of empires). In one of the great ironies of history, one of the smaller of those empires emerged and chose a Habelito shepherd youth—and not a Chenite warrior—to be their king.

Others of the Habelitos, including Selah's own great-great grandmother more than a hundred generations removed, found all of these new Chenite conceptions—production, land boundaries, and massacre—inconceivable and unbearable. The blood of the slaughtered rose up from the soil and sounded an ancient, clarion call for them to march on, to be on the move, and with the tribal yell that began every long hunt: *a-ah-ahh-ah, ah-ah-ahh-ah,* they began a thousand-year pilgrimage aimed at getting as far away from the Fertile Crescent's lunacy as possible. They followed ancient trails that had been blazed tens of thousands of years earlier by other adventurous African ancestors. These paths would occasionally fork and veer off in several directions. The faithful Habelitos awaited Elegguá's signals at each fork in the road, until the playful god finally led them to a mountain range in Asia's upper northeast corner, where they would roam and hunt and herd its abundance of reindeer. They decided (with Eleggua's blessing) to stay in this corner of earth, carving out a home on the range in the shadow of the Ural Mountains.

It was here in one of valleys on the west side of the Urals that Selah entered the world, cutting her eye-teeth on reindeer jerky as a tenth-generation mountaineer, developing skills of animal husbandry and survival in the harshest of environments. Selah had learned, like all her Habelito family, to befriend the majestic deer, relying on them for survival. She had mastered the artistry of transforming pelts into clothing, footwear, and tents. She also knew how to butcher meat and preserve it in the permafrost ice cellars. But recent years had seen the reindeer numbers declining, as many of the creatures were seen splitting off from the herd and venturing south, pushed by increasingly challenging winter conditions that saw temperatures dipping lower and lower, extending and staying well below zero (F). For the sturdy Habelitos, it was not a fear of freezing, but the prospect of hunger that ignited in some of them the ancient impulse to be on the move again, to look for a horizon that hitherto only existed in their archetypal dreams—soft, green pastures for the animals to graze, still waters for them to satisfy their thirst.

Which brings us to that Tuesday morning conclave of tribal elders who for days had been fiercely debating the pros and cons of staying and going. Centuries of mountain life had created a strong sense of home, no matter the increasing challenges posed by the changing climate. The mountains made them who they were; their identity was Ural through and through. But something else was also found to be still pulsing through Hábel veins; the driving fire of adventure, of the long march toward unexplored worlds. That flame had never been fully extinguished.

So what would it be, establishment or exodus? Selah had spent her days *not* engaging in the debate, but fasting and praying, as was her custom whenever major decisions were required. The gods would speak. She would hear them in the remote depths of her being. Three days came and went with only beckoning growls from a hungry stomach breaking the deafening silence from the pantheon. It was mid-morning on the fourth day when she heard a voice outside her tent, a strange voice—was it a man or a woman? No, it was a child, beckoning her to *come out, now.*

Selah was in the middle of preparing a morning merienda for her second born, a three-year-old daughter whose cries for deer jerky (like her earlier cries for mother's milk) had always sounded to Selah like the baby was singing. The bell-like voice always carried a melody line, which had inspired the toddler's name, Chanticleer (Chanta for short). The infant's music had helped ease Selah's long-held grief at the premature death of three other offspring before the difficult birth of the son who lived, whom she named, still being in the throes of depression, Amaro (Bitter One).

The busy mother called out for the visitor to wait just a minute. Three times the voice repeated the call, with the same words, *come out, now,* and three times she gave the same reply. When the salty, leathery stick of streaked meat and the wet-nurse milk which had been warmed over the morning coals finally satisfied Chanta's demands, Selah rose to open the tent flap and meet the child who had been calling her, but no one was there. She scanned the small community of tents, and the only person in sight was her older sister, standing outside of her nearby tent. Upon questioning, Sister said she had not seen anyone, nor had she heard any voice.

Selah immediately understood; the gods had sent her a message. It was Elegguá, the sometimes mischievous, child-like god who had brought them out of Africa and had blessed the opening steps to every long hunt ever since. He was now teasing her with a game of hide and seek. *Come out, now.* She discerned the divine message as a call to leave, to start the march, to exit this home base that had sheltered them for long enough, and to seek out another, heretofore hidden world. Chanta would provide music for the journey. Selah took a deep breath and walked into the tent of meeting. When the elders saw her, they fell silent, awaiting the last word.

As you may have guessed, that last word turned out not to be so much a *word* as it was a primal scream, *a-ah-ahh-ah, ah-ah-ahh-ah,* which soon became a chorus of shouts summoning courage from Shango for the journey to who knows where. Well, *we* now know. They travelled South, to one new world after another. For a thousand years they marched, stopping here and there along the way to establish multi-century roots, only to be up-rooted again by one pressure or another, inspiring another shout, another pilgrimage.

Along the way their identity evolved. There was the friendly encounter with another set of pilgrims, the fishing and boating Guana tribe, along the coast of what later Christian conquistadors would name Trinidad. These were the people who taught Selah's great-great-great grandchildren the delights of making love in a canoe (among other things). The Guana contributed their great skill of sea navigation, which led to another meeting of mutual satisfaction when their boats took them to the shores of the richly-flowered "bone key," the southern-most tip of what would later be christened "Florida." It was here that they met the Hatabey, a gathering clan (without the possessive nature of the Chenites), who taught yet more generations of Selah's progeny the curative properties of many leaves and roots as well as the delights of drinking floral teas sweetened with tupelo honey.

So it was that Hábel lost his name (at least in this part of the world), as the tribe's history melded into that of the Guanahatabeys (as those two clans had melded into one). This conglomeration of people with diverse and complementary gifts were the first to cross the ninety-mile channel and reach the coast of what they called "Cuba" (a name whose etymology is lost, so we can only guess that it means something like "paradise"). This would have been around 5,000 BCE. The Guanahatabeys sustained a dream-like perfect balance in this paradise for roughly four and a half millennia, living in cool caves when they found them, not-so-cool tents when they didn't, bringing together all the abilities of their respective family histories—hunting, herding, canoeing, fishing, curing. There was not a worry in the world, until the next group of explorers, the Ciboney, landed on the eastern shore in 600 CE.

The Ciboney were an island-hopping shell and ceramic culture who constructed primitive homes, called *barbacoas*, in small villages of a few families each. Their initial encounters with Guanahatabey were not hostile. But when the Ciboney began dabbling in elementary agricultural ventures, forging tools from shells and attempting to convince Guanahatabey folk to join them in the sweat-of-the-brow breaking of ground that was much harder (and unnecessary) than anything they were accustomed to, an alarm sounded. Hábel blood recognized Chen blood, and this recognition led the former to move on, always maintaining a safe distance from the Ciboney.

Unless you have done your own research into Caribbean anthropology, you might well be confused now. You may have read about or heard people talk about the Taíno tribe being the first inhabiters of the island (as well as introducing the virtues of baseball and the vices of tobacco). It is true that the Taíno were the people Columbus encountered when the Niña, Pinta, and Santa María sailed the ocean blue and made landfall at Gibarra on Cuba's northeastern coast. But the Taíno had not gotten there first; they could only lay claim to be the Third People to reach the Greater Antilles, arriving around 1300 CE, not quite two centuries before Columbus. The Second People, the Ciboney, had arrived seven hundred years earlier.

The Taíno, like the Ciboney, were Chen people, only more advanced. They wasted no time in beginning construction projects, erecting rectangular *bohios* and establishing villages. They began slashing and burning swaths of forests, replacing the arbo-culture of old-growth hardwoods and royal palms with the agri-culture of cultivated fields, a practice that would be intensified by the Europeans and eventually drive many indigenous species of flora and fauna to extinction.

Along with learning construction and cultivation, the Taíno had learned another new thing in their long journey to Cuba's paradise: they need not do all the heavy lifting, and they need not waste energy trying to convince inferior folk to do it for them. They found that their technological prowess (i.e., weaponry) afforded them the ability to force labor on others, and the hapless Ciboney had the misfortune of being those "others." Eyes and ears of Guanahatabey spies witnessed this development, from a safe distance, as another novel concept edged its way into paradise: *slavery*. As enslavement was not at all a part of the Guanahatabey constitution, the First Peoples did the same thing their Jordan Valley ancestors had done ages ago; they gave a hoop and a holler and high-tailed it; their multi-millennia knowledge of the island allowed them to stay at least one step ahead of the westward-expanding Taíno civilization.

In the two centuries of island rule they enjoyed before Columbus' arrival, the Taíno, with the Ciboney in tow, expanded their version of civilization as far west as the region later christened "Santa Clara" by the Franciscan friars. When Columbus returned to Cuba on his second journey, he reached beyond the expanse of the Taíno world, as he made it all the way around to the western half of the island. There he and his entourage finally encountered the Guanahatabey, who by this time had retreated to the caves found along the coast from Matanzas to Pinar del Rio. The conquistador's Taíno translators were not able to decipher the language of these primitive people who had not come to appreciate the value of established village life. They appeared content, satisfied to satiate their hunger with the abundance of mangos and mussels and mushrooms found in and around the bay, and to quench their thirst with herbal teas sweetened by nectar stolen from the bees. The bread of anxious toil was not part of their diet.

The conquerors were not content to co-exist with what they deemed a "savage" people (this was the word used to describe the Guanahatabey by the otherwise native-people-defender and Dominican priest, Bartolomé de las Casas). The Europeans had already overwhelmed the Taíno and the Ciboney with their superior technology, forcing them into the dreadful and deadly work of mining, via the Christianized euphemism "encomienda," which justified slavery as a divine instrument of conversion to the Christian faith. The "savage" Guanahatabey were not to be converted.

You may have read or heard about the famous resistance movement led by the Taíno *cacique*[3] Hatuey, who upon capture in 1513 was given the opportunity to receive Jesus Christ as his personal savior and secure eternal life in heaven with all the saints. Chief Hatuey was tied to a stake and was just moments away from being burned alive when the Franciscan friar shared with him the good news: "God loves you and has a wonderful plan for your life." The basic doctrines of sin and salvation, heaven and hell, were all quickly explained. The chief asked the friar if there would be any

---

3. i.e., *chief*.

Spaniards in that so-called heaven. "Of course we'll be there," replied the evangelist. Hatuey was quick to respond: "Then I want no part of it. Light the fire, I'd rather take my chances in hell."

While this episode is the best known and most celebrated act of resistance in the New World (there's even a Cuban beer named after Hatuey), it was not the first such act by native peoples against European conquest. That historic event came two years earlier, 1511, in Matanzas Bay (the deepest in the Caribbean). A group of thirty mail-clad conquistadors wanted to get from one side of the bay to the other. They conscripted a group of Guanahatabey fishermen to carry them across. Once in the middle of the bay, one of the Guanahatabey, Sheo (a name that once meant Friend Who Lends a Helping Hand, but in recent years has come to denote something that is dated or out of fashion), gave a signal, and each of the fishermen, on cue, capsized his canoe.

Sheo's signal had actually been a shout to the deity Africans would identify as Yemayá (the shortened form of Yeyé Omo Eja, mother of all and goddess of the deep blue sea). Their act of resistance was actually a prayer, in hopes that these crazed and ill-clad creatures would be welcomed back into the eternal womb, perhaps to be born again with more agreeable traits. All save one of the Spaniards quickly sank to the depths of that watery womb. The lone survivor, who had not been sporting his full metal jacket, was able to swim to shore, and lived long enough to tell the tale to Bartolomé de las Casas, who recorded it in his history of the Indies.

It is not clear whether the name "Matanzas" (Spanish for "slaughters") refers to that incident and the death of the conquistadors, or to the brutal retaliation that followed. The Spaniards scoured the deepest recesses of every cave to find objects on which to direct their fury. Guanahatabey children were captured and sent east for mining work. Few, if any, ever made it to the mines; those not succumbing to disease took their own lives, partaking of the prohibited mushrooms—not the hallucinogenic psilocybes but the lethal *Amanita Verosa*, aka death caps—that could be found by the trained eye when walking along the eastward path. After consuming the fatal fungi, in the time spent waiting for Oyá to usher them into the next world, they would begin a chant with lyrics eerily similar to one that would be used in resistance movements centuries later—*before I'll be a slave I'll be buried in my grave.*

For the adults who did not get sent eastward toward the mines, a different fate awaited. Some of the men were hung and others (including Sheo) were drawn and quartered, while most all of the women (including Sheo's life-mate, Syla) were brutally raped. While sexual violence had long existed among all of the various Chenite civilizations that had emerged around the world, *rape* was yet one more new concept that had never entered the imagination nor the lexicon of the Habelito, Guana and Hatabey peoples.

Some of the violated women found themselves great with child, with many committing suicide, aborting the pregnancy in the process. Others, like Syla, decided to give birth before ending their own lives. Picture the young, copper-skinned, short-statured, formidable woman hiding away alongside a subterranean river in the saturnine cave just east of what is now the city of Matanzas, enduring hours of excruciating birth pangs in silence until the final push, when she unleashed the last word, or rather the last shout of her life. It was the piercing primal scream that Guanahatabey mothers had used throughout the ages to launch infants on the great journey from the womb to the world. *A-ah-ahh-ah, ah-ah-ahh-ah.*

This newly born baby boy would be guided by the breath of Oyá, who aside from being ruler of the winds, is gatekeeper of the portal between the living and the dead. From what happened next, we can surmise that Oyá must have willed for this boy to live, closing her portal after giving passage for Syla to enter the world of the dead. Another breeze from the deity had brushed up against someone else who was present at the scene, a woman you might describe as a Spanish version of Pharaoh's daughter. She was one of the relatively few Old World females in the New World, having stowed away on a boat in Columbus' fourth and final journey. She happened to be there at the mouth of the cave to witness it all.

The breath that blows where it wills caused a strange urge to rise within this woman, a desire to rescue the motherless child lying helplessly by the river's edge. She took him in her arms, gave him a name, Amaranto (One Who Will Not Fade), and carried him out of the cave to be raised among the Spanish. This act ensured that the First People would not completely fade from history, as Amaranto's blood entered into the veins of history before the genocide of the Guanahatabey, along with that of the Ciboney and Taíno, was complete.

From her facial features, skin tone, shortness of stature, and core values, Sila Reyna Cervantes is bound to bleed Guanahatabey blood. I don't know how the advertised ancestry tests work, but I'd wager that her genetic results would demonstrate some kinship, however slight, with the hunting and gathering and fishing and tea-drinking Guanahatabey. Her two last names, of course, tell us more of the story, revealing as they do some DNA strands from a Spanish heritage. On her father's side, she carries the apellido *Reyna,* making her "queen Sila." The appellation speaks of her deep dignity, her settled nature, and her strong rule of life. Were she to actually be enthroned in some imaginary kingdom, her reign would flow from a Kantian ethic of obligation based squarely on the concept of divine and neighbor love. For Sila, love is the law that regulates every aspect of life. Maybe her kingdom isn't so imaginary after all; you wouldn't be far afield in describing her pastorate of the small flock at her baptist church in La Vallita as that of a benevolent and beloved queen mum.

Then there's *Cervantes*, from her mother's side, perhaps putting her in a genetic line shared by the famed creator of the man from La Mancha. This also fits her character well. Sila definitely has a quixotic side; she is utopian, romantic, idealistic. And she has tilted at more than one windmill in her quest to bring justice and fairness to her community, always acting in solidarity with the underdogs. Add to that her continued full-throttled participation in and support for Cuba's revolutionary project, including her leadership in her neighborhood's Committee for the Defense of the Revolution (CDR), which would probably lead critics of that system to conclude that she is a dreamer of impossible dreams (note: the CDR is the butt of many sarcastic jokes among those who find the system and its committees more offensive than defensive).

One of those critics once shared a popular dissenter's joke, not aimed at the CDR but at the system in general: "God granted every nationality two gifts at birth (art and cuisine to the French, for example). When God got around to the Cubans, three gifts were bestowed: intelligence, honesty, and a belief in communism. Other nations immediately cried foul—why do the Cubans get three gifts, while everyone else gets two? God replied, 'Not to worry, a Cuban can only have two of the three at any given time. If you are intelligent and honest, you can't be communist. If you are intelligent and communist, you can't be honest. And if you are honest and communist, you can't be intelligent.'" Laughter at the joke died down when someone lifted up the example of Sila Reyna Cervantes, exhibit A in evidence that all three attributes can indeed co-exist in one person.

To paraphrase a line from *The Tempest*, what's past is prelude, literally *pre-drama*, before the play. And to quote another of the bard's famous lines, "the play's the thing." Part of that *thing*, the thing that makes the play of life so dramatic, is the seemingly universal tension within human beings between staying and going. The ancient past of Africa, Asia, and the Americas, connecting the lives of women like Selah and Syla, women who struggled with that creative and crazy-making tension is, for the purposes of this book, prelude to the drama (sometimes comedic, sometimes tragic) of women like Sila. The rest of the book will follow this format, with meandering stories mixing fictional preludes of people who ventured out into the wider world with factual accounts of the their descendants who are enacting the Cuban drama now. Be it fact or fiction, it is all true, as true as I can make it.

La Vallita
Friday, June 22, 2012 CE
6:15 p.m.

I love remembering an encounter a group of travelers had with Sila Reyna back in the summer of 2012. Her intelligence was on full display in a way that came as a surprise, if not a shock, to some of the first-time visitors to Cuba, especially a young pastor. We endured the long van ride, made the five hundred step walk, and arrived to wipe the mud off our shoes before entering the home sweet home of Sila and family. Like most of the *casas* in the community, hers is a simple, concrete-block building of maybe 600 square feet, with a living room, kitchen, bathroom and two bedrooms squeezed into that limited space, which doubles as sanctuary for the church. Add to this simplicity of design the lack of any running water in the house (the toilet is flushed by a bucket of water brought in from the well), and by North American standards, it is quite the humble dwelling.

So imagine this young visiting pastor's jaw dropping when, after the initial meet and greet, Sila launched into an enthusiastic description of the thesis she was working on for her degree at the ecumenical seminary in Matanzas. It involved an analysis of Jürgen Moltmann's theology of hope, and how it would apply to a rural church in Cuba that is developing an open and inclusive stance toward LGBTQ persons. "What? We're here on a dirt road in the middle of the Cuban countryside, in a house without running water, and this woman is riffing on German theology? What's more, how many gay people could there be in La Vallita?" (I'm imagining what might have run through the pastor's mind at the moment his jaw dropped).

That last puzzling question that might have been in the pastor's mind, about the presence of non-heteronormative folk in the macho culture of Cuba, was easily answered by Sila with one of her life stories. This genesis of her interest in advocating for justice and respect for people regardless of sexual orientation happened when she made a visit to the neighboring town of Florida to visit her mother in the hospital. Sila had gone to the highway to flag a ride, and used all of her disposable income, ten Cuban pesos (equivalent of forty cents) to pay the driver of the converted cattle truck who stopped to take on the passenger. She spent a few hours at her mom's bedside, and as evening approached, she walked back out to the highway, without a clue how she would get a ride back with no money in her purse.

She sat on a bench near the park and started praying for God to send her an angel to get her back home. A stranger came and sat next to her on the bench. Sila didn't know him, but deduced from his mannerisms and from the conversation that he was gay. He showed genuine compassion about her mom's condition, and promised to keep a good thought. An *almendrón* (one of the beat up old classic cars used as private taxis) stopped to see if either needed a ride. Sila knew she didn't have the $1.50 fare, so she just shook her head, no. Her bench-mate walked up and talked to the driver, and then motioned for Sila to get in the car; she had a ride. She explained her plight, and he said not to worry. Sila got in and learned from the driver that the young man had paid her fare. God had answered her prayer, sending her a gay angel to get her home. That was enough for her to decide she needed to open her eyes to the angels unawares all around her, and sure enough, they do live in La Vallita.

Also on that same church trip in 2012 were my brother Jerry and his grandson, Tommy, a nineteen-year-old first-year college student. Tommy brought the assigned summer reading for one of his classes, the novel *Ishmael* by Daniel Quinn. I was delighted; this was a book I had used in a college class I had taught years earlier. Tommy was equally fascinated by the book and by the Cuban experience, filled with curiosity and questions about both. As the purpose of trips like these is friendship-building (we don't build churches or dig wells or do other "mission trips" service projects), visits to La Vallita involve a lot of time sitting around, drinking coffee, and conversing. So Tommy and I had quality time to talk about *Ishmael*; he particularly wanted to find out what I thought about the gorilla's interpretation of the Cain and Abel story in Genesis (the protagonist of the novel is a genius gorilla named Ishmael). This was my favorite part of the book, and had prompted me to ask a lot of people the same question.

The primate professor's thesis was that the Cain and Abel story represents the larger story of human history and what was going on in the Fertile Crescent ten thousand years ago. It was then that the Chenite (Cain-ite) wing of the Fertile Crescent family began developing settled agriculture, creating surplus food and social stratification. In so doing, they found co-existence with the nomadic hunters and herders contrary to their plans, and thus began slaughtering the shepherds, driving those who survived to the margins of the emerging civilization of Semitic society (Cain is represented in the Biblical story as the father of cities, i.e., of civilization).

I engaged Sila in the conversation, and she was equally intrigued by the interpretation. She, like most readers of the Genesis story, had always been puzzled by God's rejection of Cain's offering. From professor Ishmael's perspective, this particular chapter of the biblical story echoes the voice of the ancient animal husbandry community, who felt divine blessing on their wandering way of life, and presumed divine judgment on the established way of life in the cities. Their voice rose up from the ground.

Sila took particular pride in her family identification with the Abel community—elder son Amaury milks cows for a living (he has the forearms to prove it); before that he had a job midwifing piglets into the world and raising them in the first months of their lives. His younger sister Anabel worked for about fifteen years with those same piglets turned fattened hogs at the other end of their lives, at a slaughterhouse. That's not to say the entire family was Abel-oriented; Sila's spouse, Cheo, manages a sustainable agricultural cooperative, bringing grain (and fruit and vegetable) offerings to the tables of La Vallita.

I like to get Sila to tell some of her life story to groups who come to visit. That small group in 2012 learned that she arrived in this world in 1948, born the first of eleven children in a barrio called Don Eduardo, part of the countryside of the Camagüey province. She is proud to be pure *guajira*, the Cuban word for country bumpkin. The roots of the pejorative nickname, one that has become as commonplace in usage as "redneck" in English, speaks to the inherent prejudice that "civilized" people have for people living outside their bounds of privilege. When Sila explained the etymology of *guajira* to us, I shared how words like that, and worse, are sprinkled throughout the English language. *Villain, pagan, heathen, delinquent, vagrant*—all these words have their roots in words that originally referred to people living outside of the city, people who chose not to comply with the codes of Cain's civilization.

Guajiro, she explained, came into the lexicon during Cuba's third and finally successful war of independence against Spain in the late nineteenth century. When the US found an excuse to intervene at the end of the war, sending in knights to save the day, the shiny-armored Cavalry saw the ill-clad and poorly armed rural *mambises* on their puny horses, and poked fun, pointing at them while shouting "War Heroes!" The true heroes, this rag-tag band of rural rebels who had suffered years of grueling battle against the colonial forces, did not quite understand the English, nor the pun. They thought it was some kind of affirmation, and their Spanish language ears heard the pronunciation *Guajro*. The appellation stuck.

In our coffee and conversation time, we talked about how in some sense we are all children of Cain, living as we do in a civilized world. Few of us would survive if we were to be plopped down in the midst of one of the surviving authentic hunting/gathering nomadic communities, in Papua

New Guinea or the Tibetan mountains or the Lacandona jungle of southern Mexico. We all agreed that there is much to appreciate about Cain's contribution to human life: pop culture, plumbing (primitive as it may be in La Vallita), iPads (Sila's grandchildren have not avoided the seduction of video games).

The diversity of offerings in the established world are endless; there's something for every taste. Just within our little gathered group in La Vallita, Cheo looks for the opera on tv when he gets home from plowing the fields, while Amaury relaxes with Prince Royce videos when he gets home from milking the cows. Sila loves traditional trova; Anabel's tastes run toward nueva trova. Kim listens to Beethoven and Barry Manilow, while I immerse myself in the Beatles and Silvio. Tommy is into hip-hop while his granddad Jerry prefers doo wop. But whatever our cultural leanings, wherever our travels take us, all of us are always on our way either to or from Canaan-land (Cain's land).

Having an appreciation for settled civilization and having an attraction for its cultural treasures does not negate another attraction we have in common, the unsettling call to escape the establishment and be on the move. The blood of Abel rises up from the ground, through our feet and into our hearts. Sila loves sharing stories of her various travels; the pilgrim's urge was always strong in her, starting in childhood. Her first forays into the world beyond hearth and home were short ones. They came when she was old enough to accompany her mother on the two-kilometer journey to the river, the water source for campesinos in the Don Eduardo community. There was also a lagoon that some families used, about the same distance from the *bohío*, but Sila preferred walking to the river. Its never-ending current and flow fascinated her. The water seemed to be alive.

So for those who knew her well, it came as no surprise when Sila started the church there in the living room of her home in La Vallita and named it Rivers of Living Water Baptist Church. She was inspired by her favorite hymn—*Yo tengo un gozo en mi alma. . . es como un río de agua viva..* (I have a joy in my heart. . . it's like a a river of living water). In talking about her childhood, she is quick to warn us against romanticizing those daily pilgrimages to the river. While the spectacle of the running water was truly captivating and mystical, the work itself was grueling, carrying water home for drinking and cooking, carrying clothes to the river for washing. She is forever grateful for the progress afforded campesinos by the Revolution, such as having a well in her front yard and a 1970s model Russian washing machine in her back yard.

Speaking of grueling work, Sila's family, along with the other families living in Don Eduardo, were the labor force for the finca Santa Sofia

(Saint Wisdom). The tradition in the countryside was for children to join that force at an early age (having many children came in part from the illusion that many hands would make light work, but the work load never lightened). Sila does not remember ever hearing her parents say why they broke with this tradition and gave her the rare opportunity as a rural child to attend the poorly-attended primary school. Perhaps the infinite wisdom of the farm's Saint Sofia inspired them. At any rate, she was the first in her extended family to learn her letters.

These letters would provide the reason for her first trip away from home. In 1960 Fidel Castro, fresh from winning the final battle against the Batista dictatorship, traveled to New York and stated (among many other things) in a speech at the United Nations, "Our pueblo intends to wage a great battle against illiteracy, with an ambitious goal of teaching reading and writing until the very last illiterate person has been taught, all in the next year." The revolutionary fervor and enthusiasm for changing the world was palpable, as two hundred and fifty thousand people answered his call and volunteered for the campaign. More than one hundred thousand of these, including Sila, were under the age of eighteen (she had just turned twelve when she volunteered).

This campaign has been widely covered in books and documentaries, but most of these focus on the brigadistas who ventured out from Havana and other cities to travel to the countryside and bring literacy to peasant communities. Sila wants to make sure people remember the role of families like hers, country people who agreed to serve as hosts for the young urbanites who knew nothing of rural culture. The history books all teach about the ultimate sacrifice made by Manuel Ascunce, one of the literacy workers who was shot and killed in April of 1961 by counter-revolutionaries who were still roaming the mountains, intent on undermining the Revolution. Sila wants to make sure the sacrifice of Pedro Lantigua is counted in the history as well. He was the father of the family who hosted Manuel Ascunce, and when he tried to protect the young teacher, he was killed, too.

The tremendous courage of both brigadistas and the families who hosted them is underscored when you remember that in that same month of April, not many days after the murders of Manuel and Pedro, the US launched an attack on Cuba, at the Bay of Pigs. Sila recounts that these acts of aggression did nothing more than fortify the will of the people to continue their work. Sila's own family volunteered to participate in the campaign, and hosted Ruth Reyes, a young girl of Sila's age who came from Guara, a municipality of Holguín, two provinces away. Ruth and Sila, both bright fifth graders, taught together at her family's kitchen table.

The campesinos of Don Eduardo who came to that table were counted among the seven hundred thousand Cubans who learned to read that year. But one person stands out to Sila; she gets teary every time she tells the story of teaching her grandmother and two of her uncles to read. And then her tears turn to laughter as she recounts her first trip away from home, accompanying new friend Ruth Reyes on a visit home to see her family. They mounted the *gauaga* (the Cuban word for omnibus) and found it to be a relatively smooth ride on the recently constructed carretera central, which had not had time to collect all the potholes the years have since contributed to the highway. When I think of twelve-year-old Sila making her way from the simple homes of the countryside and seeing a city for the first time, I can't help but remember an experience of her granddaughter Ruth Vivian when she was but a young girl of six or seven.

It happened in 2010, when we arrived in La Vallita with a church group, stopping by Sila's house before making our way on to our hotel in the town of Florida, about thirty minutes away. Ruth Vivian wanted to accompany us to the hotel and help carry our luggage in. We checked in to the hotel, and started up to our second story room. Ruth Vivian was carrying one of Kim's bags, and when she reached the top of the stairs, she stopped, looking out over the railing. She had this frozen look of amazement in her eyes, and when I asked her if everything was alright, she exclaimed, "Tío, I've never been this high before. Look how far you can see!"

I don't know if young Sila got to climb any stairs and see the world from a different perspective when she went to Guara. She did experience one "first" there, though. Ruth Reyes' older brother, fifteen-year-old Agustín, developed a crush on Sila, and started sending her love letters. Nothing came of it, as she felt he was far too old for her, but it does bring out a twinkle in her eyes when she talks about her first romance. She kept up her friendship with Ruth for several years, and then lost touch, until more than thirty years later when Sila's father was diagnosed with cancer and had to travel to Havana for surgery. Who emerged to be the surgeon but Doctora Ruth Reyes! She was so glad to be able to repay the family for the generous hospitality and friendship they had shown her so long ago.

For Sila, the experience of teaching her elders to read was the awakening of her vocation, not into medicine like Ruth, but into teaching. At age fifteen, she was ready to embark on her training with another trip away from home, combining studies with practical teaching experience in the Escambray mountains of the Sancti Spíritus province. This was particularly challenging, as the Escambrays were one of the hotspots of counter-revolutionary activity; this is where Manuel Ascunce and Pedro Lantigua had been murdered. Another challenge, this time from nature—Hurricane

Flora—cut her time in the mountains short. She and her fellow teachers in training were transferred to Varadero Beach in the Matanzas province, the same place where the brigadistas had been trained for the literacy campaign (currently one of the premier tourist destinations in the world).

At age sixteen she began her second year of training with another trip, this time farther away from home to Minas de Frío in the remote Sierra Maestra mountains, the very place where Fidel Castro had mounted the Revolution. Soon after the triumph of the Revolution, Che Guevara established a pedagogical training school there. In Minas de Frío, Sila and her fellow teachers-in-training slept in the open air in hammocks and taught classes under the shade of the ceiba trees. She continued expanding the options of what impoverished peasants could do with their lives. The sky was the limit; they could stay and work the land (a noble calling), and some did, but more discovered other, long dormant callings to become doctors or dentists or lawyers or engineers or ballet dancers or opera singers.

Sila then went west, traveling the entire length of the island to complete her training at the tender age of seventeen, teaching in a primary school in the Havana municipality of Bauta. Her assignment: a group of second graders, all from broken homes, all with emotional disturbances and severe disciplinary problems. Nothing in her formation had prepared her to deal with students like Bárbaro Chávez and Pablo Figueroa. The youngsters were determined to break her, and they were successful; she began waking up with the nagging question that many teachers face at some point in their career: "should I stay (in bed) or should I go (to work)?" "Should I stay here in Havana, on this career path, or should I go back home and find my place on the farm?"

The budding teacher's question was answered for her when she suffered a nervous breakdown and had to take a leave of absence from her beloved profession. It was in her time of recovery that she realized an important truth: she was stronger than these youngsters were; she was smarter; she was wiser. And she realized that what they needed was love and guidance. She went back to the classroom, and Bárbaro and Pablo and their companions had the great blessing of Sila Reyna Cervantes' presence in their lives, loving them, believing in them, finding the key to their own sense of identity and calling and purpose in life. Years later these boys, who had grown into men, would seek her out, proud to tell her of their successes in life, and grateful for her part in their journey.

I imagine worlds colliding when I think about Sila's journey in her late teens. Her arrival in Havana came just before the appearance of another young woman whom she never met, but with whom she had a lot in common. Margaret Randall, New Yorker by birth, had made her way to Cuba from the

Black Mountain Folk School, a haven for hippies and poets and avant guard artists that was located just about fifteen miles from where I grew up.

Margaret, like Sila, was a poet, loved literature, and admired Fidel Castro. She had heard him make that same famous speech at the UN, and like her young Cuban counterpart, had been inspired by the call to end illiteracy across the country. Margaret Randall spent ten years in Havana, hanging out with the very writers that Sila loved to read, Nicholas Guillén, Cintio Vintier. I can imagine what it would have been like had these two young women met. I can hear Sila reciting Martí poems, along with some of her own. I can hear Margaret Randall sharing how she had seen the proverbial canaries dying as US culture continued to mine the depths of capitalism, heedless to its dangers, so she had fled to breathe safer air.

Unlike Margaret Randall, Sila only spent one year, not ten, in the *capital de todos los cubanos*. After that final year of practice teaching, she graduated with honors and began her full-fledged teaching profession, landing a position in the small town of Florida, not too far from the countryside of Don Eduardo where she grew up. She was happy to be closer to family, and to her delight, was assigned a class of adolescents (an age group she was far more comfortable with) at the Julio A. Mella Middle School. Once again, though, all of her students came with disciplinary problems. The entire class had failed the previous year, and were repeating seventh grade.

The principal of the school asked Sila what subject she would like to teach, and her response was "anything except mathematics." They gave her Spanish literature, and being an avid reader as well as an aspiring poet, she was ecstatic. She remembered the lessons learned from Bárbaro Chávez and applied them to her work with the ring-leader of these misfits, Nelson Pérez. He had earned the nickname Nelson *Reguero* (a disorderly mess, a wreck), as his constant defiance and mischief left a wake of disarray in his path. Something deep down in Sila assured her that as the adult in the room she would have the last word, and she quickly applied some psychology on the Reguero. She made him her assistant, giving him important jobs to help her out, playing on his ego needs to be leader of the pack of hellions. It worked; Nelson tidied himself up and "led" all of his classmates to be successful students.

At the end of the school year, the middle-schoolers had the tradition of bringing gifts to their teachers. Sila was in the teachers' lounge with several of her colleagues when a somewhat red-faced Nelson Pérez came in, holding a gift, poorly wrapped in newspaper. He handed it to her and ran off. Sila opened it, and to her fellow teachers' amusement, she held up a pair of bloomers! They all started to laugh and poke fun, but Sila stopped them, saying that she could not have received a more meaningful gift if it had come from Fidel Castro himself. She was proud, because she had been part of this youngster's transformation. He, and all of his fellow students in that troubled class, passed their end-of-grade tests, and moved on to eighth grade. The principal could hardly believe it.

Sila had many such success stories in the years that followed, but her professional triumphs were offset by a serious and traumatic personal failure. She had married and given birth to her first child, a son named Amaury, only to find in her first year of motherhood that her husband was prone to infidelity. He abandoned wife and son to follow his passions, leaving Sila depressed and in dire straits. She was down to her last two kilos (pennies) with almost no food in the cupboard. A second nervous breakdown was crouching at her door, and in the depths of that hellish threat, she decided to give God a shout.

Never having been a religious person, Sila knew very little about matters of faith. Nonetheless, she improvised the first prayer of her life: "God, I'm going to give you a shot. I only have two kilos to my name, and need to buy some food. I'm going to put these pennies down on the *bolito* (an underground numbers racket long popular in Cuban culture), and if I win, I'm all in for you." She went to local lottery man on the corner, placed her bet, and as luck (or God) would have it, she picked the right number and won enough money to put food on the table for a week. Keeping her end of the bargain, she gave her heart and soul to Jesus.

Not knowing what to do with this conversion, she waited for Sunday to come and walked into a worship service at the first church she passed, a hell-fire and brimstone, shouting and fainting, holy-roller Pentecostal variety. While not knowing exactly why, something inside told her this was not her style. Sila is big on the values of José Martí, Cuba's famed "Apostle of Independence" and he was big on being "cultured" (one of his most famous sayings is "being cultured is the only way to be free"). Something about the noisy and unwieldy worship of the Pentecostals seemed to her to be on the uncultured side. The next week, she tried out a little Baptist congregation in the home of a neighbor; there she encountered a relatively quiet, orderly, and thoughtful liturgy, and that same internal voice told her this was the real deal. She had discovered home.

The years passed and the family grew, as Sila met the second love of her life, Cheo, and their marriage soon produced her second child, Anabel. Being at "home" in church and in one's family does not always mean paradise, though, and Sila soon experienced brokenness in both. She and Cheo's marriage wound up on the rocks and they separated. At the same time, she experienced some pushback from the church around what she was teaching in her Sunday school class (she was beginning to sense a call to ministry, and this class was her first opportunity to test the waters of that vocation).

Sila had come to believe that the gospel in one word is "love," and that we could spend a lifetime trying to live out the truth of what for Jesus were the most important commandments, to love God and neighbor. When a member of her class asked for an example of neighbor love, her response was that if your neighbor is hungry and thirsty, and you have food and drink, then love requires you to share what you have. The member who raised the question was not happy with the answer, as it sounded too much like socialism to him, and he was on the dissenting side of the political equation in Cuba. A major conflict erupted. Sila told the congregation that if she could not freely teach the ethics of Jesus, she would need to leave.

In the ways that perfect storms work, there often needs to be a third disaster to bring about a total collapse. Along with family and church strife, the third traumatic "break" came to Sila when she was called in for her annual evaluation meeting with the local minister of education. This had always been a pleasant encounter, as she had earned the well-deserved reputation of being one of the best teachers in the province. This meeting would be different, though, for when the administrator asked for her id card so he could jot the number down on his form, another card fell from Sila's purse. It was the card of another local pastor, who had given it to Sila some time back when she had sought out someone to pray for her. The administrator picked up the card, read the information on it, and asked Sila a simple question, "Does this mean that you are a religious person?"

Now, to understand the import of this simple interaction and question, you have to know that at this time in the context of Cuban history, the revolution was officially atheist and Marxist. People of faith were viewed as relics from an earlier era of human evolution; it was thought that once they understood basic tenets of science and philosophy, they would throw off the shackles of superstition to enter into the new utopia of scientific materialism. Sila held her head high as she answered the question, "Yes, I am a Christian, a follower of Jesus of Nazareth." To which he replied, "I'm sorry to hear that, because that means you can't be a teacher any longer. We will miss your presence in our schools. I hope some day you will see the light and come back."

In God's mysterious ways of working, it is often the failures and brokenness of life that open doors to grace and hope. At least this is what Sila came to believe. There she was again, at wit's end, a suddenly-single and unemployed mom with two small children in tow, struggling to discern a vocation to ministry but having no church family to support her call. It was time for another serious prayer, but this time with no testing of God's luck in the lottery (she had learned that much). She simply prayed for God to show her the way of escape out of the mess she was in.

The answer to her prayer came in a dream; in the dream she saw a house and heard a voice. The house was small and humble, of concrete block construction, but it was not one she had ever seen, and she had no idea where it was. The voice simply said, *Este será el hogar de su iglesia* (this will be your church home). Several days came and went, and she had no idea what to do with this mysterious vision, other than prepare herself for a journey. For the one thing she did know about the house was that it was not in the community where she lived. She deduced that God did not want her to stay; she was being called to get a move on. For all she knew, the house might be far to the west in Havana, or far to the east in Santiago. Or, it might be in Timbuktu. Wherever it was, she was ready to go.

Some days passed and her brother called, saying he had some business to do in a town about forty-five minutes away, wondering if she would like to go along for the ride. Sila had heard of the small pueblo of La Vallita, but had never visited. When they got there, her brother turned left off the central highway and drove past the old folks' home on the dirt road, then turned right to get to the house where he had some business to conduct.

To Sila's shock, they passed by a house that seemed strangely familiar, and on second look, she realized why. "This is it! This is the very house that showed up in my dream!" No one was at home, but they discovered that the house was indeed for sale, and the woman who was selling it now was living back in Florida. The neighbor gave Sila the woman's first name and an address where she could be found. They drove back to Florida, found the direction and knocked on the door. Another shock—the woman who answered had been a friend of Sila's several years back; they had taught together for one year.

Her old friend was delighted at the prospect that Sila might buy her home and move to La Vallita. Sila asked the price, and her heart sank when the woman told her it was ten thousand Cuban pesos (the equivalent of $400 USD). Sila had scraped and saved over the years, and all she had was half of that amount. With tears starting to flow, she thanked her friend and said she only had half that amount, and that there was no way she could come up with the rest. When she turned to leave, she heard her old friend cry out, "Wait!" She turned back and could hardly believe what she heard next. "Something tells me you are supposed to have this house. I will sell it to you for five thousand pesos now, and whenever you get the rest, you can pay me then. No rush."

Sila gathered up the youngsters and without a stick of furniture moved into this new dream home. The first thing she did was to start the first baptist mission in La Vallita (she had made peace and reconciled with the home church, which became the sponsoring church for the mission). The first convert in the mission, and the first person pastor Sila baptized, was none other than her repentant husband, Cheo, who grew in faith to become an amazing and trustworthy helper in her ministry. Following Cheo in the baptismal river were the two children, fifteen-year-old Amaury and twelve-year-old Anabel. The family, and the church, were once again whole.

I first met Sila when Kim and I visited her mission in La Vallita on my first trip to Cuba in 1999. We both fell in love with her, her family, her congregation, and her community. While I couldn't articulate what it was about her that did a job on me (for the longest time I simply called it the "Cuban magic"), I think I now have a better idea. She is at once deeply rooted in her place, bringing the kingdom of heaven to earth in this little rural community, and at the same time as free a spirit as I've ever met. The Reyna in her lives out the best of Cain (she is a civilizer if I've ever met one), and the Cervantes in her lives out the best of Abel (shepherding her flock, ready to roam in search of still waters and green pastures if the need ever arises).

So it was that when her mission reached the stage of development to be commissioned as a church, and our little church in Fairview was looking for a Fraternity of Baptist Church to form a long-range partnership, we knew it was a match. In 2010, the two congregations officially joined themselves at the hip and began the exciting and hard work of learning from each other, which as much as anything meant unlearning millennia of destructive mission models between over-privileged and under-privileged cultures. We (on the over-privileged side) are still learning the lesson, over and over again, but I trust that Sila has the same patience with us that she had with Nelson Reguero, and the same fierce and determined love. One day I expect we will make the grade and finally pass this particular test of life.

Part of our learning has taken place at our home in Fairview, where we have hosted Sila on three occasions, giving her a chance to experience sabbath rest beside the still springs of the western NC mountains. She was one of the fortunate few Cubans who was successful in her visa application during that short window of time in the Obama administration when those who did get approved received a multiple-entry visa good for five years. While I can vouch that she enjoyed her times of rest up on the mountain, it would not be appropriate in her case to say that the Good Shepherd had led her to green pastures, as she is not counted among the Cubans who imagine that the grass is greener on the other side of the ninety-mile waterway.

At any rate, it was on her second trip, in the fall of 2011, when we stumbled into a deeper friendship. I realized early in her visit that I was suffering from an embarrassment of riches. Our home, by US standards, is a humble one, but by La Vallita standards, we might as well have been living in a Trump Tower. I constantly found myself wondering, "Why do we need so much stuff, and so much space?"

I couldn't quite share these feelings with Sila, as I was at that time woefully inadequate in my Spanish, but I had learned enough standard phrases to make small talk. In one of these small conversations I thought it appropriate to spit out the phrase I had seen on so many billboards in Cuba: *Hasta la victoria siempre*. She looked at me, a bit stunned, and asked, "So you know Che's *despedida* to Fidel?" I confessed that I did not, that I had only seen the phrase on so many posters underneath Guevara's iconic head-shot. "What's a *despedida*?" I naively asked.

A side note before getting to her response to my question. The Spanish word for "remember" is *recordar*, which in its etymology originally meant "to pass through the heart again." Sila has an amazing memory, which is to say, she has many things passing through her heart time and time again. Che Guevara's letter to Fidel is one of them. She proceeded to recite word for word the entire lengthy letter that the Argentinian doctor turned guerrilla warrior wrote as a farewell (*despedida*) to his friend and commander in chief in 1965, when he left Cuba to incite and support revolutionary struggles in the Congo.

Che had left an important post in Cuba's Revolutionary government— he was in charge of industry—but two things (at least according to some historians) prompted him to ask himself, "should I stay or should I go?" He landed on the answer that he should go. One reason, as the maxim tells us, revolution is easier than governance, and at least for Che, that was true. He was a revolutionary, not a government minister. And second, he was not happy with the Cuban leader's decision to cast his lot with the Soviets. Che felt they were just another empire, talking the talk of socialism but far too dictatorial and far removed from their base. He was a believer in the people's rebellion, and wanted to foment an authentic Latin American form of socialism, not be a puppet of a superpower on the other side of the world. So he left.

When Che left, he penned his goodbye to Fidel with words of encouragement for the Cuban leader to be true to the principles they had fought for, to stay the course they had dreamed of, and his signature line gave us the words he is now famous for: "to the victory always." It was in 1968 that Che found himself hiding out in the mountains of Bolivia, strategizing with Bolivian rebels how to avoid the mistakes and repeat the successes he had experienced in Cuba. The Bolivian government had zero experience in dealing with guerrilla warfare, and called on the US government to help. The

CIA agents sent to respond to the request did have experience, and eventually were able to locate Guevara's camp.

The agents had him assassinated (leaving it to a Bolivian military leader do the deed). When photos of the dead body of Ché Guevara reached Cuba, Fidel gave a characteristically long speech in memory of the fallen warrior in the Plaza of the Revolution. With his famously dramatic flair, Castro ended the eulogy in a crescendo with the closing line from Che's letter, *Hasta la victoria siempre.* Suddenly, the CIA had not taken out a revolutionary, they had created a martyr to the cause, complete with an iconic slogan that would cheer on the Revolution for decades to come.

My chance repetition of the line and Sila's giving me the historical context led us to deepen, or enlarge, the small talk we had been accustomed to. She had not been 100 percent confident she could share her values with us; after all, we were US citizens, not many of whom have any affinity at all with socialist revolutions. In fact, her time in Miami, where she had to fly in and out to get connections to NC and back to Cuba, put her in the presence of people who gave her a genuine fear for her life; their rancor and hatred for the Revolution was so palpable. She was delighted to learn that she could be herself around us; that she would be respected for her values and political leanings, and maybe even could find some kindred spirits there in the backwoods mountains that in some ways reminded her of the Minas de Frío.

Not long after this game-changing conversation, I helped Sila make a Skype call to talk with her spouse, Cheo, and let him know how things were going. I'll never forget one line of her phone call—"Cheo, it's great here. Kim and Stan have a lot of really sophisticated stuff, but it hasn't ruined them." It was as good a blessing as I've had in my life, one I hope I can live into.

It was also on this second visit to the US that Sila had the opportunity to go into some schools and make presentations about life in Cuba. She had great fun dancing the rumba with some Latino kids in the public elementary school where Kim was teaching English as a Second Language. Then, she was able to engage in dialogue with some students in a private, church-based high school civics class. After finishing her presentation, Sila gave the students an opportunity for q&a and conversation.

The first question left her a bit perplexed: "What is it like to live under a dictatorship?" Later, she told me that what first ran through her mind as she formulated an answer was "have you not been listening to anything I've said so far?" What she did say was something like, "I'm not sure what you are referring to when you say 'dictatorship.' I imagine that's how your history books here and your news accounts describe our political system in Cuba. But it's not the case. We elect our president, who happens to be our beloved and historic leader of the Revolution."

A follow-up question came: "But you only have one political party; what's the point of voting?" To which she gave a bit of a mischievous smile and replied, "I'm not sure the quality of a democracy should be measured by how many political parties you have to choose from. Were that the case, the US would be far behind most countries in Latin America and Europe, because you only have two, while most other countries around the world have five or six. Now you wouldn't say that means their system is superior to yours, no more than yours is superior to ours because you have one more party, would you? To your point about why bother, I vote because I want my voice to be heard. But more importantly, I have found there are many ways to get engaged in the political process to improve our communities, and voting is just one of them."

Next question, "Does that mean you are communist?" She paused a moment and gathered her thoughts. The question, and its tone, reminded her of the question her administrator had asked her upon seeing that she carried the card of Christian pastor. "Does that mean you are a religious person?"

Sila wondered what consequences might come from her answer here, and she also wondered just how deep into the complicated world of political theory she wanted to go with these teenagers. Here's where she dove in: "Well, no, I am not communist," and then it was her turn to leave them perplexed: "and for that matter, our country is not communist." She waited for the looks of confusion to set in before clearing things up. "You see, communism is the ideal, the dream, the utopia we are all hoping to see one day. Socialism is the system which works to achieve that utopia. Socialism is what we have in Cuba, our means to reach the ideals of communism."

Another question, "What does your dream, your utopia, look like, and how will you know when it's there?" Now that's a good question, Sila thought. "I think we'll know we're there when everyone has enough and no one has too much, like the Bible talks about." Eyebrows raised and hands shot up in the air. Sila pointed to one of the eager students, who asked, "Where is that in the Bible?" Sila asked if any of them liked the book of Proverbs, and several said yes. "Me too," she said. "It's a wonderful book to prepare people for leadership, in whatever political context. Chapter thirty in particular speaks to me about my hopes and dreams for Cuba, in the verses where the wise writer shares his prayer to God: "Give me neither poverty nor riches, but give me only my daily bread. Otherwise, I may have too much and disown you and say, 'Who is the Lord?' Or I may become poor and steal and so dishonor the name of my God."

Back in 2012, Sila could have taken an easier route when asked if she was a Communist. She could have simply said no. Her answer would change a few years later, though, when another set of teenagers got to hear the story behind the change. A group of twenty US youth and twenty Cuban youth, along with some adult chaperones, were making a choir tour from one end of the island to the other, singing and learning and having fun along the way. Sila had been charged with organizing a meal for them all in La Vallita, at one of the carretera central roadside restaurants where the *guaguas* (buses) regularly stop for a lunch break on their cross country trips. Sila excitedly told me she had a story to tell, and I was all ears as we sat down to eat. A few of the US teenagers were sitting with us and overheard the tale.

Just a couple of weeks prior to our arrival, she had gotten a call from the Party (i.e., Communist Party) headquarters in Florida. They said they needed to come by and see her. This made her a bit anxious, and she wondered what she might have done to raise the ire of Party officials, or at the least to be on their radar. Two officials showed up on her porch at the appointed hour (more or less on time), and she gave them the same hospitality she offers every visitor. They quickly got to the point. "We have been hearing about you for some time," one of them began.

Sila tensed up, but was soon set at ease. "We hear that you are behind virtually everything good that happens in this community. You are in the vanguard of every improvement. We have heard about the blood drives, the projects you have organized with parents to help the school, we could go on and on, but we will get to the point. We want to ask you to join us." She paused, and asked for clarification, "You want me to what?" The second official repeated, "to join us, to join the Party."

"But," she replied, a bit confused, "I am a Baptist pastor." She laughs when she recounts their come-back to that confession, "We know, but we won't hold that against you." They talked a bit more, and Sila ended the conversation by saying she needed some time. This was something she would need to pray about. She asked for three days to decide. She spent those three days in prayer and fasting, as she always did when a major decision was needed. She was sure the Lord would give her a word, a sign, as to what to do.

She was still waiting on the afternoon of the third day, hungry in her body, and even more hungry for that word of the Lord. She was in the back of the house hanging up clothes on the line when she heard a knock at the door, and a one-word shout, "Family." She yelled back for the visitor to wait just a minute as she finished hanging the sheet on the line. Two more times the visitor knocked, each time with the same word shouted out, "Family," and each time she responded that she would be right there.

She got to the door, opened it, and no one was there. She scanned the dirt road, and saw no one. Her neighbor across the street was in her yard, and Sila asked what happened to the man who had been knocking and yelling. "What man?" The neighbor asked. "I've not seen or heard anybody." Sila immediately knew what had happened. Jesus had just paid her a visit. And given her a message. "Family." But Jesus was being mischievous, or maybe playful, with her. "Isn't it just like the Lord to give you a message wrapped up in a mystery, and you have to figure it out?" She asked me. She spent some more time in prayer, seeking some discernment about how to decipher the message. It came to her, and it all made sense. "We are all family. The people in the Party, the people in the church. We are all trying to do what families do, survive, thrive, make things better. There need not be these false divisions." She called up Party HQ, and gave them her answer. "I'm in."

Sila was proud to tell me and the others at the lunch table that day that she was both a card-carrying Christian and a card-carrying Communist. Maybe the only one in the country. For her, it's not about politics or ideology. It's about God's love, incarnated in another poor *guajiro—Jesús de Nazaret*—a long time ago. For her, it's all about Emmanuel, God with us.

Chapter 2

Walking with Orestes and His Spanish Ancestors

Por muchos lugares pasaba la historia.[1]

—Silvio Rodríguez, Por muchos lugares

Matanzas, Cuba
Monday, May 5, 2020 CE
8:30 a.m.

Whereas it takes ten hours by bus or van and then five hundred footsteps to reach the door of Sila Reyna Cervantes, I am not likely to wear out much boot leather on the ten-step journey to the kitchen door of Orestes Roca Santana. Orestes, our next-door neighbor and as close to a blood brother as I could imagine having in Cuba, is Senior Pastor of First Baptist Matanzas (going on twenty years in that role), father of seven-year-old Lucas and five-year-old Marcos, dean of the ecumenical seminary where he teaches Greek and New Testament studies, and is working on his PhD. Given the intense stress of that combination of responsibilities, his spouse Wanda recently asked me for a favor: to find opportunities to talk with Orestes about rock and roll. Any topic other than something work-related

---

1. Translated: "History passes through many places." Rodríguez, Silvio. "Por muchos lugares." Érase Que Se Era (Vol. 2). Ojalá, 2006. Album.

would do, but she knew that we share a particular affinity for the fine points of rock. No problem, can do.

Orestes is a born conversationalist, and can *dar cuero* with the best of them (*dar cuero*, literally "give leather," is the Cuban phrase for engaging in biting, wickedly funny satire). It wasn't satire that had me laughing this morning, though; it was his song choice providing the soundtrack for his breakfast—Deep Purple's *Highway Star*. I heard the music coming from the kitchen while I finished watering the plants in the Kairos Center and made my way up the two flights of stairs back to our apartment.

I made the short-cut ten-step journey from our home to theirs, the second step being the dangerous one. To avoid having to descend those stairs and go out the Center door to then enter their door and climb a different set of stairs to get to their house, we have become accustomed to stepping onto the narrow ledge and swinging a leg over the meter-high concrete wall that serves as a planter for Wanda's orchids, crocus, oregano, and aloe, then swinging the other leg over to land on their patio, and then taking the other eight safe steps to enter their kitchen. This morning the smell of coffee wafting onto the patio mixed in with the screaming voice of Ian Gillan that had made me smile—"I can drive with power, big fat tires and everything. . . alright, hold tight, I'm a Highway Star."

Orestes, who neither has a car with fat tires nor a license enabling him to drive with power, could nonetheless sing along as a consummate fan and student of classic rock. I took the opportunity to launch into a story about the short-lived but glorious mid-seventies era of eight-tracks, when a local radio station put out the invitation for listeners to call in and vote for what they deemed to be the best eight-track to have playing on a road trip in a muscle car with a six-pack in the back (listeners could also weigh in on what was the best muscle car and the best beer while voting on the best eight-track). Deep Purple's *Machine Head* won hands down; I agreed with the results that nothing could top cruising up the Blue Ridge Parkway in an Oldsmobile Cutlass Supreme with some cold PBR singing along to *Highway Star* or *Space Truckin'* (although we would soon get more than our fill of the over-played *Smoke on the Water*).

I have always considered myself a classic rock aficionado, but Orestes proved early on in our friendship that in terms of rock and roll knowledge he is the teacher, and I am the student. It was 2013 and he was visiting our home in the mountains. As luck would have it, the Cuban National Baseball team was on a friendship tour, playing a team of US collegiate all-stars in various venues across the country. There was a game on the schedule for play in Durham during the time Orestes was with us, so we got tickets and made the four-hour drive to get to the Durham Athletic Park.

I had made that I-40 trip many times, and had discovered where on the radio dial all the classic rock stations are along the way. We decided to have a contest—name the song and the artist at the start of each song. I don't know how many different selections the deejays spun out on the various stations during that four-hour trip; what I do know is that I only managed to beat him to the draw once. He was amazing, not only knowing song titles and artists, but lyrics, and background trivia about the various groups, be they big names like Metallica and Pink Floyd, or lesser-known groups like Judas Priest and Mountain. He explained that rock and roll had been his schooling for English as a second language.

I would definitely have kicked myself if I had not achieved my one victory. The brass section had barely started their intro when I blared out, *Caves of Altamira!* Steely Dan! I might be a second-rate aficionado of classic rock, but I might as well have my own PhD on the music of Becker and Fagen's Dan band. I had immersed myself in jazz when rock and roll as we knew it died (from the double blows of disco and big hair bands), and it was Steely Dan who kept me connected to the genre. Once I discovered the jazzy arrangements and mysterious lyrics of *Aja,* I went back and bought every album, copiously studied every guitar riff, and read every article on the group that came out in any music tabloid.

I waffled over the years as to what was my favorite LP, but I kept coming back to *Royal Scam.* Elliot Randall's and Larry Carlton's guitar mojo has stood the test of time, classic from start to finish. I shared with Orestes the story of having had a chance encounter with Elliot Randall back in my teen years, hearing him demonstrate a guitar in a small kiosk at a music merchant's convention. I had not realized who he was until the next issue of *Guitar Magazine* had a photo of him playing in that same kiosk; I couldn't believe that I had missed the chance to chat up a session player about his work with Steely Dan (was that solo on *Reelin' in the Years* improvised or planned out?). And I explained to Orestes how John Klemmer's sax solo on the song we were listening to, *The Caves of Altamira,* ranks up there with Phil Woods' *Just the Way You Are* solo as about as good as it gets when jazz crosses over into the world of rock.

I ended the stories in time to sing along in the richly harmonized chorus: "Before the fall when they wrote it on the wall when there wasn't even any Hollywood, they heard the call and they wrote it on the wall for you and me, we understood." Orestes was happy to hear the stories and learn some trivia about my favorite band, and then during a commercial break from our contest, he stumped me with a good question (which reminded me that I may know a lot about the group, but I am not a know-it-all). "So you know about the caves of Altamira, right?"

He wasn't referencing the song, but its basis. I had to confess that I did not (I would have googled it back in the day when I was so immersed in their music, but the world wide web had not yet arrived on the scene, and I was too lazy to go to the library and do my research). No problem, this gave my friend the chance to assume his role as teacher and fill in some of the gaps in my cultural knowledge. Orestes is a born teacher; this is what connects all of his different roles and responsibilities. He could have been the poster child for my seminary professor Wayne Oates' book, *The Christian Pastor*, in which the pastoral care giant argued that the stack pole on which all other pastoral duties lean against is teaching.

Cave of Altamira
Cantabria, Spain
Monday, May 11, 14,500 BCE
8:30 a.m.

It was the first class of the day for the students who lived and worked (hunted and gathered) in what would later be called Green Spain, named for the lush grassland surrounding Mount Vispieres on the northern border of the Iberian peninsula. Professor Oros Histeim, whose name in the pre-Proto-Indo-European language spoken by the tribe meant *Standing Mountain*, was indeed an imposing figure, not only because of his height, but also due to his lofty grasp of truth and virtue. In the Altamira school, held there in the 1000-feet-long halls of the cave carved into the limestone mountain by eons of karstic phenomena, there was but one fundamental field of inquiry: *meaning*, which was comprised of the sub-fields of aesthetics (beauty) and ethics (duty).

It would be a common mistake to name "spirituality" as another course of study. Neither the professors nor their students would have understood the concept of spirituality, as it was such an ever-present constant in their lives that they were not even aware of its existence. These proverbial fish had never been out of water. That the words "spirituality" and "religion" eventually came into the human vocabulary signified the species' fall from the true Way, and their attempts to recover that Way. But Oros Histeim and his students lived, as the song tells us, "before they fall, when they wrote it on the wall." Well, before the *complete* fall.

The plush valley land in the shadow of Mount Vispieres was not the paradise of Aganju and Yeyé at the Cross River watershed in 80,000 BCE. The Green Spain hunters and gatherers might not yet have experienced life outside of the Spirit, but they did understand that the concept of *beauty* signified the possibility for something to be *not-beautiful*, i.e., ugly. Life was not always elegant. And they understood *duty*, a concept which signified that there was the possibility of *not-duty*, i.e., irresponsibility. Shoddy work existed.

As for the subject of beauty, the cavernous Grand Hall just past the covered entrance provided a phenomenal space of study. Measuring sixty-feet long by thirty-feet wide, and with a low four-foot ceiling, it would lead today's learners to liken the classroom experience there to that of studying aesthetics while lying on a high scaffolding in the Sistine Chapel. The cave's ceiling had been used as canvas for generations of Michelangelos who mixed charcoal and ochre and hematite to paint incredibly sophisticated polychromatic images of bison and other steppe animals. Painting was not exactly Oros Histeim's forte, so he left the finer points of design principles and technique to other members of the tribal faculty. His passion resided in the exploration of truth and virtue that lay behind the symbolism tribal artists had painted on the cave's wall and ceiling over a twenty thousand year period.

For professor Histeim, part of the task of understanding the wall's messaging lay in understanding history. Being part of a long line of oral historians, his knowledge went back at least as far as those twenty millennia of human life in Green Spain. He knew that he was not the only Standing Mountain to have spent time in the cave; the first human to arrive had started the journey at the Cro-Magnon mountain in Dordogne, France. Over the millennia, other Standing Mountains had made the descent from the towering Pyrenees. He knew their history as well. He also knew that before the early artists ever took to painting bison and deer and horses, they engaged in what looks to the modern viewer as abstract art, etching and painting geometric symbols whose interpretation has yet to reach consensus among the anthropologists trying to decipher them.

Oros Histeim would no doubt laugh heartily were he to hear some of the prevailing theories that modern researchers have put forth as to the meaning of the abstractions. The flaw in modern research has a two-fold basis: for one, the cave was closed by a landslide in 12,000 BCE, and would not be rediscovered until late in the nineteenth century, so the moderns do not benefit from the unbroken line of oral history and knowledge of the cave that gave Oros his edge. And secondly, perhaps more importantly, there is the flawed assumption of "human progress" in contemporary research, an assumption that leads to the foregone conclusion that the ancient humans, "cave men" in popular lingo, lacked capacity for abstract thought. The symbols, so the reasoning goes, had to have some very basic, very primitive and practical purpose. The leading theory is that these etchings, along with other examples of the onset of written language discovered around the globe, were nothing more than accounting tools for managing inter-tribal trade of livestock and grain.

Bean-counting was about as far afield from Oros Histeim as one could imagine. He was, in today's terms, a philosopher, a priest, a mystic. In his day, he was simply a truth-teller. And for him, as well as for all the Standing Mountain shamans who came before and after, the theoretical and the practical sides of truth were woven tightly together. A large part of the schooling was to prepare for the journey, for the hunt. The Great Hall was not, however, the place students came to learn how to kill and butcher an animal, that was field-learning. The classroom focused on the more important matters.

Oros was basically reinforcing the deep truths of animism that had been inherited from their most ancient African ancestors. Understanding and having faith in the animating sacred force that inhabits everything, every plant, every animal (including the human animal) and every rock, this was the core faith of his tribe and of all the tribes that had preceded them. The cave's walls and ceiling, filled with both abstract and realistic art, served as the scripture for the millennia of tribal hunters and gatherers who found their way to Green Spain.

If you were a modern day physics professor and had the opportunity to sit in on a class there in the Cave of Altamira, you would possibly be surprised to see some similarities to your field while hearing this sacred text read and interpreted by teacher and students. A pre-requisite for being on the hunt was to know what the physicist would call the 1st Law of Thermodynamics, or the Law of Conservation, which tells us that energy is a constant; more of it cannot be created, neither can any of it be lost. In the physics texts, the geometric symbols used to explain this law and its implications would obviously look different than those on the Altamira wall. Thirty thousand years from now, discoverers of our texts would face similar challenges trying to make meaning and decipher the formulaic messages of Δ and Q and δ and W.

Oros Histeim's challenge as he sat in the great frescoed hall with his twenty students, was to explain how the etched lines were showing how we are all connected to the great life force, the great energy, and this energy never fails, never dies, never ceases to be, it simply moves from one shape to another. When a being, like a powerful bison, "dies," it simply transfers its life energy to another form, and continues on the journey. Death, then, is something to be respected, not feared. Were Mount Vispieres or the Pyrenees to suddenly crumble into the sea, it should not inspire terror. The energy, the force, is still there, just in a different form.

Professor Histeim would move from the abstract etchings to the herd of bison on the ceiling and explain the truth in a more spiritual, less scientific way: The bison herd, like everything else, is a part of the great divine, the sacred force, the life energy that animates the universe. The bison represents, or more precisely animates, the magnificent strength of the divine force. The bison, to state the obvious, is greatly superior in strength to that of the human. Our species animates the weakness of the sacred energy, its vulnerability. We need to manufacture protection from the elements, in the form of fur coats or boots. But the bison, what a tremendous force—not only in its sheer strength, but in its capacities—it has built-in protection from the elements. And it has the capacity to consume the green grass (which in itself animates the life force of the sun and the soil) directly, without mediation. Our species, on the other hand, has to go to a lot of trouble to process the protein (or rely on the animals as delivery-devices) so our systems can receive the transfer of energy.

The human capacity, by contrast, is in the hands. Moderns who take it as a given that the larger brain is what differentiates humans from other creatures lack the advantage of having lived in the time when the Neanderthals faded from earth. These extinct beings had larger brains and thus more complex brain functions than did Einstein and his fellow physicists. Oros Histeim knew that it was the homo sapiens' superior hands that made up for smaller brains and gave his species the staying power. He could wax eloquent for hours on end about the wonders of the human hand, and the many ways the hands animated the divine energy at work in the world. Some of his Semitic counterparts in the Fertile Crescent would one day compose songs about this divine handiwork—"the heavens declare the glory of God and the skies proclaim the work of sacred hands." Some would see justice meted out by the right hand of the divine force, while still others saw the sacred energy of the left hand animating the sinister side of God.

Oros taught his students that their shared connections to the gods meant they all belonged to one another, they were etched into one another just as the symbols and bison images were etched into the mountain rock. His "final exam" was for them to prepare a prayer liturgy before the great hunt, in which they would place their hands on the cave floor, blow a mixture of ochre and hematite dust around their hands to create a relief image. These prints would become praying hands as the students petitioned for the divine in them to recognize the divine in the bison. They would give thanks to the member of the herd who would be sacrificing life to them, and would pray for the great spirit to guide their hands in finding the right animal, the one who was prepared to lay down his life for them.

Scholars of religion would do well to research just how and when this concept of sacrifice was reversed in the development of diverse spiritual traditions. Long before faith communities sacrificed burnt offerings of bulls and sheep and goats to God or the gods, the hunters and herders of old believed that the real liturgical offering involved God sacrificing part of the Divine self to the humans, in this case transferring the sacred bison energy for the sake of the vulnerable. Perhaps one of these sociologists of religion would raise a question of the Jesus crucifixion narrative, wondering if the early gospel story-tellers were echoing or channeling something of the Altamira theology of sacrifice.

In the final weeks of his life, when Oros Histeim knew he was dying, the professor came close to weeping when he got to this final lecture of his annual course. "This, this is meaning," he would say. "We are all etched into this mountain, this great rock that animates the solid, constant force of life, that has its roots in the fire far below and reaches up to the heavenly fire." So it was that his students, as a last homage to their beloved instructor, prepared the ochre and hematite dust, helped him through the cave's halls to find the perfect place, and prayed with him as he placed his hands on the wall. The students one by one took turns etching the stencil of the aged hands, and then they all blew the dust to create the relief. Dust to dust, rock to rock. His final "assignment" was for them to return to that spot every year before the hunt, and to remember that the divine spirit of Vispieres was in them all, not just in one like him who was named Standing Mountain.

It would take many millennia for the descendants of Oros Histeim to take that spirit of Vispieres with them in journeys beyond the range of the great hunt. Some would settle in Catalonia, others in the Canary Islands, and still others in Castile-León. And from there, the spirit would blow them yet farther away from Green Spain, as first one and then another boarded ships sailing for a new world, making landfall in Cuba, where marriages and children and grandchildren would eventually produce not an Oros, but an Orestes.

Orestes Roca Santana, when he is not talking about rock and roll, loves to engage in conversation around the Bible, movies, and history, not necessarily in that order. He used to have more time for movie-watching and commentary, but parenting seven-year-old Lucas and five-year-old Marcos has limited his film consumption to the occasional late night or Sunday afternoon (nap time) offering. Even with these limitations, my own repertoire of cinematic fare has greatly expanded from being around Orestes, as the movies he does happen to catch run far beyond Hollywood; I have been introduced to some great foreign films. One of the funniest (though probably not considered so great in an artistic sense) that we watched together was a 2004 French comedy, *Rrrrr*, set in 35,000 BCE, with the plot revolving around the conflict between two competing clans, the Clean Hair and the Dirty Hair. A murder prompts the first ever police investigation in history. I have my doubts that the film-makers did any research that would create the most remote resemblance between these tribes and real pre-historic cave dwellers like those in Altamira.

Regarding the topic of history, a typical morning of sharing coffee at the kitchen table might start out with my asking a simple question, "Where does the name *Orestes* come from?" And I get to learn about its etymology that goes back at least as far as the ancient Greeks and means "One Who Stands on the Mountain." My professor/pastor/friend/brother/neighbor appreciates the irony of carrying such a tragic name, first made famous in Aeschylus' fifth century BCE dramatic trilogy *The Oresteia,* which dealt with murder and revenge and the reaction of the gods. His namesake comes to the fore in the second play, *The Libation Bearers* when young Orestes comes back to town to kill his mother and her lover, who had killed his war-hero father. The contemporary Orestes would appreciate the appropriateness of the play's title, seeing as he does the morning ritual of coffee-making something of a drink offering poured out to the deity (there is actually a Cuban expression about coffee being the black nectar of the gods). The short answer to my question is that a third-cousin who left Cuba after the Revolution and now lives in the US is named Orestes, and his grandmother liked the sound of the name.

A brief side-note: I am always amazed at Kim's capacity to remember things. When I told her about this conversation with Orestes, she immediately launched into a passage from Aeschylus' *Libation Bearers*, a scene she had learned in a theater class forty years ago! "Oh, the torment bred in the race, the grinding scream of death and the stroke that hits the vein, the hemorrhage none can staunch, the grief, the curse no man can bear." She continued, making a stage out of our little kitchenette, and concluded the scene with dramatic flair: "We sing to you, dark gods beneath the earth. Now hear, you blissful powers underground—answer the call, send help. Bless the children, given them triumph now."

The Cuban Orestes also knows another historical footnote to his name, as it was an unfortunate namesake who gained fame for being at the helm of the Western Roman Empire when it fell to the marauding hordes from the north in 476 CE. All it takes is a mention of that kind of historical trivia, and suddenly Orestes can light up and start describing a longer and more nuanced history of the Iberian Peninsula, of which the Romans coined the name "Hispania" during their time of imperial rule there. While he doesn't connect all the dots in his description, I get the message from the long over-view that we humans need to be a bit more humble when considering our systems of governance and rule. Words like "siempre" (always) and "jamás" (never) don't really apply to human institutions, something the Caesars and all others like them would eventually learn.

Those original tribes of hunters and gatherers who found their way to Green Spain and its surroundings would have had the most right to think in terms of always and never, as their nomadic way of life, their fairly uncom-plicated manner of governing themselves, was the most sustainable known to humankind, lasting roughly thirty thousand years. During those tens of millennia, numerous regional tribes crossed paths and coexisted, including Celts, Iberians, Celtiberians (a mixture of the two), Tartessians, Lusitanans, and Vascones. Then came the Yamna, around 3,000 BCE, whose DNA re-veals they came in large part from the Caucasus Mountains.

These Caucasians changed everything, having chosen, like their Chenite counterparts had done in the Jordan River Valley five thousand years earlier, to give up the simple life for a more complex civilization. That is, they came as conquerors. Perhaps the contemporary Caucasian tendency toward a white guilt complex has its roots in this unfortunate choice of the Yamna. These peninsular civilizers (who also happened to have domesti-cated the horse) created a social and political infrastructure sophisticated enough to manage large herds attached to settled agricultural develop-ments, and as it happened in every part of the world, the settled life inspired dreams of expansion and conquest.

The Yamna experiment at taking over the peninsula ended after a couple of thousand years when their Greek counterparts rose to power in the world and expanded their rule to what they called Iberia. Their con-quest lasted seven hundred and fifty years, followed by the Romans with four hundred and fifty years of rule, the Goths with three hundred years, and the Muslims for two hundred and seventy-five years (this was the era of Convivience, with Jews, Christians, and Muslims living together in relative peace). The Convivience was followed by two hundred and fifty years of battle over the territory, ending with the Christian reconquest, which lasted two hundred and twenty-five years, during which time Velázquez painted and Cervantes wrote. (Note how the illusory "forever" fantasy of each suc-cessive rule keeps getting shorter and shorter.)

The reconquest led to the unification of "modern" Spain under the the Catholic monarchs Isabela and Ferdinand (the patrons responsible for Christopher Columbus finding his way to Cuba), and they were followed by one hundred and eighty-five years of Hapsburg rule, one hundred years of Bourbon rule, and then there is a long line of short-lived revolutions and back and forth trading of power. The twentieth century experience of forty-five years under fascist Franco's rule must have seemed like an eternity to Pablo Picasso and others who suffered from his atrocities, but in reality it took no more than one generation to transfer power to the constitutional monarchy of today's Spain.

On one of those rare mornings at the breakfast table when the boys were still sleeping, Orestes and I were talking about Spanish history (or rather, I was asking questions and he was teaching) and my professor enthusiastically found a scrap of paper on which he sketched out a map of his ancestral home country. "Today's Spain is actually a conglomeration of seventeen different autonomous kingdoms," he explained, and started placing these ancient kingdoms on the map: Cantabria (home of the famous cave), Catalonia (where his paternal ancestors had settled), the Canary Islands (from whence one line of his maternal ancestors hailed), Castile-León (home base for the other maternal line), Galicia, Castile-La Mancha, Andalusia, Aragon, Basque Country, and so on. "Up until fairly recently, they each had their own language, and still today the Basques and the Catalonians speak their distinct mother tongues, which explains some of the separatist/independence movement."

As these dreams of conquest and establishment and power were pulsing through the veins of first one kingdom and then another, there were always subjects in those kingdoms whose hearts pumped out another set of dreams, fantasies of escape from the establishment, of being on the road, free to explore new possibilities. I asked Orestes if he knew why his ancestors left peninsular life, why they crossed the ocean to wind up in Cuba. He laughed and said, "Most everybody who left were poor, marginalized. The rich, the establishment elite, they had no reason to leave. But my forebears, they were struggling, hungry, tired of the boot on their neck, wanting to find a better life. Of course the other reason some came was to fight in the war, but all the same, the Spanish didn't recruit their elite to go off soldiering in some remote island colony. Once the war was lost (from the Spanish point of view), many of these soldiers chose to stay and cast their lot with the Cubans instead of going back to the hard life they knew awaited them."

If the ten-step journey to meet Orestes at the kitchen table brings many such conversations around history, longer walks produce even more talk, richer and deeper. Sometimes I accompany him on his walk up to the ecumenical seminary, where his second job awaits. We start out on Calle Medio (Middle Street), as the church and home is located there in the middle of town, between Zaragoza Street and Santa Teresa Street. This is enough to provoke a bit of theological riffing, given that Zaragoza is a reference to Caesar Augustus, while Santa Teresa alludes to the sixteenth century Carmelite mystic. Orestes thinks this is an appropriate locus for him, exercising leadership in an established institution (First Baptist Church) while at the same time being drawn to the discalced life of simplicity and silence.

From this mid-point between Caesar and the Saint, there are two ways to walk to the seminary, and Orestes prefers the 1,070-step route along Zaragoza and then Manzaneda that leads to the back gate, over the 1,120 steps it takes to ascend Dos de Mayo (a street named for a rebellious uprising) and enter in by the front gate. It's not the fifty-step savings that he prefers; it's that Zaragoza is an easier walk. Hiking up Dos de Mayo is uphill all the way (most rebellious uprisings are), while Zaragoza is level until you cut over to Manzaneda, where you have a short but steep climb to get to the back gate.

You can imagine that the pilgrimage to the seminary would provoke conversations around matters of faith, spirituality, the Bible. The first time I remember walking there with Orestes was back in 2011, when I was doing a series of podcast interviews with pairs of people who shared a similar vocation, one in the US and one in Cuba. On this occasion, the Cuban half of the pair was ninety-six-year-old René Castellanos, aka Maestro. He was a founding professor of the Matanzas seminary, having earned a PhD in languages at the University of Havana as well as having done graduate work in psychology at Columbia University. Add to that resumé a lifetime of study of folk dances from around the world, and you come up with a true character.

Maestro's US counterpart, Walter Harrelson, was a language scholar as well, having led the translation team for the New Revised Standard Version of the Bible. Dr. Harrelson, five years younger than Maestro, was living in the same retirement community as my in-laws, so I got to visit and chat with him regularly. It was a unique blessing to be something of a mediator of a long-distance conversation between these two nonagenarian giants who each had cut wide swaths in the field of religious education, but had never crossed paths personally.

While I had a fixed set of questions I asked in each interview, I took advantage of my time with these two to pick their brains about a Biblical matter that had been on my mind since my college teaching days: the interpretation of the Cain and Abel story in the novel *Ishmael*. What did they think of the hypothesis that this Genesis account reflects what had happened in the Fertile Crescent in 8,000 BCE, that it was describing the conflict that arose between the ancient nomadic culture and the newly emerging establishment culture? The answers I got from both were confirming of the idea, but in very different and fascinating ways. Maestro Castellanos, with his formation in depth psychology, spoke of the archetypal pre-history stories as revealing the internal world mapped out in each human brain, including the true internal struggle that every individual faces—whether to be on the move in search of green pastures and still waters, or to stay in place and forge institutions (the "should I stay or should I go" question).

He described his own personal journeys, from Placetas to Cardenas to Havana to New York to Matanzas, with regular trips throughout his work life to Princeton and Ghost Ranch. He was as established as one could be in the seminary community, having lived and worked there for sixty-five years, but the desire for pilgrimage was always present. Dancing, he told me, that urge to move one's feet in rhythm, comes out of the early settled cultures and their nostalgic longing for life on the move. When humanity settled down and pushed the wanderers of the world to the margins, the "civilized" cultures, in every corner of the world, invented dance as a response to the need to be free, to move.

In this the tenth decade of life, Maestro Castellanos' personal impulse to pull up roots and be on the move took shape in his conversations with God, dealing with his wish to leave this world so that his spirit could take flight and dance with the angels. The answer he got to his prayer was "wait," as he discerned the voice of God telling him he was still needed there at the seminary. A different, positive answer would come to him less than a year later.

Dr. Harrelson, whose formation had more to do with archeological digs than archetypal angst when it came to interpreting sacred stories, mapped the pre-history stories in more of an anthropological direction. He directed me to numerous journal articles that dealt with the universal conflict between settled agricultural communities and nomadic shepherding tribes, which in the biblical narrative takes shape along the axis of several polar opposite tensions, such as temple-keepers versus tent-dwellers. Another tension involves the valuing of surplus good production (the Joseph story in Egypt) versus the critique of such surplus, seeing it as a vice to be punished (the wilderness wanderers' manna story).

The ten thousand-year-old Fertile Crescent experience was repeated throughout history all over the world, the professor told me, and yes, Cain's city-centered story has been dominant in every case, marginalizing the unsettled peoples. He shared how one of the many wonders of the Bible is that the marginal community (Abel's culture), although defeated, was never silenced, and the thread of this alternative movement message is woven throughout the more dominant temple narrative.

As an example, he shared with great enthusiasm some of his own research in his team's translation work for the NRSV, where he advocated fiercely for a change in the translation of Isaiah 35:8. Historically, this verse has been read as saying that there will be a highway in the desert, a Holy Way, and the unclean will not pass over it, i.e., will not journey on it. This projects the verse as being a voice from Cain's civilizing project, aimed at depreciating those who fall outside of its realm. Dr. Harrelson's research in the wording of the prophetic message led him to believe that the real meaning is just the opposite, that it is a defiant Abelite assertion—there will be a Holy Way, "and the unclean will not miss it, it will be *for them!*" For him, this was an example of the voice of the marginalized nomadic community with a message of redemption for their people who had been deemed unclean by the dominant religious culture. He lamented that he had not been able to convince the majority of his team, which was required for a major change to make it into the new version, so his reading was relegated to a footnote as an alternative translation.

Walter Harrelson and René Castellanos died within a few months of each other in 2012, the year after my conversations with them. Our encounters percolated through many conversations with Orestes on our walks up Zaragoza to the back gate of the seminary, where he would be following in Maestro's footsteps in teaching Greek and New Testament studies. I was going there to follow up on the clues I had been given, scouring the library (along with Orestes' personal library) for relevant scholarship around the early Genesis stories. My younger professor was also helping me prepare to teach these new discoveries in several different venues—the seminary's summer biblical institute, a joint retreat in Cienfuegos with young adults from our church and from Ebenezer Baptist in Marianao, Saturday popular (i.e., grassroots) reading of the Bible sessions, and Sunday School.

Connecting the biblical narrative with the historical overview of cultures, such as the Spanish history, Orestes could appreciate how the various human competitions to conquer and civilize is largely a sibling rivalry among the children of Cain. Whether it involves the Yamna or the Greeks, the Romans or the Goths, the Bourbons or Napoleon, there is always some kinship, something familiar about the attempt to consolidate power and govern a civilized swath of territory. Increasingly complex sets of regulations, like the fifty-seven laws in the Code of Urukagina or the two hundred and eighty-two rules of Hammurabi or the six hundred and thirteen Mosaic laws, replace the simple nomadic shepherding honor code, two-fold in its nature virtually anywhere you find it: take care of the people and animals within your circle, and offer hospitality to those you encounter outside your circle.

Fast forward through the thousands of years of Spanish history to its expansion into the new world and its ultimate loss of that conquest, and you can see current Cuba-US relations (and lack thereof) through the prism of the same sibling rivalry: communist child of Cain vs capitalist child of Cain. Each gets some things right, and some things wrong; the degree to which you emphasize the right or wrong of either depends on which sibling you identify with, but they both operate from the basic assumptions of papa Cain's big-city establishment story, not the wilderness-wandering Abel narrative. One point Orestes likes to make is that even with this similar basis of ideals between competing cultures, the frustrations and craziness one experiences living within either space is distinct, and understanding that madness requires having grown up within the particular system. Cubans might be able to imagine it, but they cannot really know the extent to which a materialistic society based on uncontrolled, limitless consumption can be crazy-making. Likewise, US folks can imagine but not really know the ways in which an idealistic society that controls and limits consumption can be utterly maddening.

Saying "no" to one of the siblings in this rivalry and escaping from the madness in either setting takes on different forms. In Orestes' youth, many Cubans took to the turbulent waters in whatever craft was available or could be fabricated, to seek a better life in big brother's form of civilization (Cain would be proud of the Cubans' conquest of Miami, and the resulting king-making power they enjoy in presidential politics, where Florida's electoral college votes provide them with inordinate power). For the US part, saying no to the "good life" and making an escape doesn't imply a reverse trip across the waters to give little brother a try (although you might say that is what Kim and I are doing). Making a getaway is more often seen in another kind of trip, evidenced by the widespread plague of addiction that has swept the entire country, on the majestic purple mountain ranges and across the fruited plains, from sea to shining sea.

Orestes and I get a glimpse of one of these shining seas on another of our regular walks that we enjoy, the 1,675-step journey to Pueblo Nuevo, the barrio where he was born and raised and where his mother, Esther, still lives. Before we were homebound in the COVID quarantine, this was a weekly pilgrimage to enjoy some of Esther's Sunday dinner culinary magic. We would walk the seven hundred and ten steps down Calle Medio to the Vigía park, where you can see the San Juan River emptying into the Atlantic Ocean's Bay of Matanzas. Then we would cross the river with another one hundred and fifteen steps on the Concordia bridge, and then six hundred and fifty steps on the *calzada* (two-way street) Tirry, and two hundred final steps to arrive at Esther's doorstep on San Juan de Dios. It is a fitting journey for pastor and apprentice (I was serving as his associate pastor) to make, leaving Caesar Augustus (Zaragoza) behind to arrive at a street named for a monk. On those walks, the talks often take a different turn. The nostalgia of going home provoke many stories of family and friends.

These stories are not disconnected from the larger historical themes. I observed to Orestes once that while it is true that all the big empire builders like to fantasize and promote propaganda of *siempre* (forever), only to give way to some other conquering force after a few hundred years, the people, the families, don't live in stretches of three or four hundred years. They are confined to live out their lives in a seventy-five year patch somewhere within the empire's historical trajectory of rise and peak and fall. And despite claims to the contrary, nobody really has the perspective to know exactly where we currently are on that spectrum. So no matter what version of civilization we find ourselves in, it can feel like forever. Whether you experience that feeling in a hopeful, utopian way or a depressing, dystopian way largely depends on the personal stories and the stories of your loved ones that define your life.

For Orestes, the Cain-Abel story and its tension of staying or going is mapped out via the life stories of family and friends, somewhere between Maestro's Castellanos' archetypal maps of the individual psyche and Walter Harrelson's archeological maps of competing civilizations. The community-level tension of staying and leaving hovers somewhere between the microscopic neurons that fire and wire like chain lightning every half-second and the macroscopic mega-empires that clash and shift like tectonic plates every half-millennium. I suspect there is a great deal of interplay between the three levels—these community-level tensions and conflicts have a part to play in the development of both brain circuitry and imperial struggles for supremacy, and vice-versa. Which, for me, makes Orestes' stories of family and friends so fascinating.

In his growing-up years of the 1970s, Orestes' household on San Juan de Dios street in Pueblo Nuevo included him and his parents, Esther and Papo, his younger brother Osmani, and Uncle Humberto, his father's older sibling. One of Orestes' earliest memories is of a treasure he discovered in Humberto's closet; it was a stainless steel water cup, the kind we might see in camping gear. This one was beautifully engraved with two hearts, and inside the hearts were the names Evaristo and Dulce (Humberto's parents). Outside the hearts were the names Papo and Humberto. For some reason, this metalwork was fascinating to the four-year-old Orestes, and he often went to the closet to fetch it and spend time admiring the artisanship. Many years would pass before he would learn the story behind the metal cup. It had been a gift from Humberto to his parents, one that he had made, or perhaps had someone make, while he was serving time in prison.

Humberto and Papo had worked for several years in La ChiChí, a cracker and cookie processing plant in Pueblo Nuevo, named after the wife of Clemente Mesa, the owner. The business was very successful, and Clemente had risen from humble origins to be one of the richest and most respected citizens of Matanzas. When the Revolutionary government began nationalizing industries after the Triumph, it was not just the major players like sugar and rum and tobacco and the utility companies that got nationalized. Most of these had been owned and run by the mafia or foreign interests, and Cuban people were for the most part enthused to see the change of ownership. Not so much with the small mom and pop businesses, such as this bakery that had been built from the ground up by a local poor person. People had serious reservations about this micro-level of the state's eminent domain.

Papo had found other work by the mid-sixties, but Humberto was still working at La ChiChí when it became government property. He and some of his fellow workers were not happy that the owner, one of their own Pueblo Nuevo success stories that inspired them all, had been robbed of his enterprise. To show their disapproval of what was going on in the nationalization campaign of small cottage industries, Humberto and a few co-workers engaged in some Saul Alinsky sabotage tactics, secretly throwing a wrench in the works (literally) to stop or slow production. They were soon discovered, arrested, and put on trial.

The prosecution sought the death penalty for this crime against the Revolution, but their lives were spared and they received sentences of twelve years. Humberto served four and was released on good behavior. A confirmed bachelor, he spent the rest of his life living in the home of his brother Papo and family. He never spoke of the incident at La ChiChí or the prison time. Twenty years later, Humberto came down with terminal cancer, and after some time of treatment he was discharged from the hospital to die at home. It fell to the now-adult Orestes to carry him from the car to the house, and before he made it back to his bed, Humberto died in his nephew's arms.

It was April 1, 1980 when nine-year-old Orestes watched some big news airing on Cuba's state-run television and radio. Six disenchanted Cubans had commandeered a bus and crashed through the gates of the Peruvian embassy, hoping to gain political asylum and a seek a different life in Peru. The security guards opened fire, and one guard was shot and killed in the crossfire (by another guard, as none of the six dissidents were armed.)

After some negotiations, in which the embassy refused to hand the culprits over to the Cuban authorities, Fidel Castro declared he was removing all security from the embassy, as the Peruvians were harboring criminals and not cooperating in their own security. Upon hearing this news, many thousands of Cubans, with similar disenchantments and desires to flee, made their way onto the embassy grounds and occupied it.

It was a disastrous situation, as the occupiers not only included the serious dissenters longing for the day when Cuba would revert to its 1940 constitution or become the fifty-first US state or convert into something akin to that; there were also otherwise decent people who simply wanted to go and reunite with family members, as well as a sizable number of rabble-rousing ne'er-do-wells wanting to take advantage of the opportunity. Within five days the situation had devolved into a serious humanitarian crisis. The Cuban government provided some food, but not enough to go around, so hunger abounded and the roughnecks of the crowd made sure they got the first portions. Fights and bedlam ensued, and the less-than-noble sector of the crowd was what typically made the airwaves on the nightly news.

Recalling this event brings another memory to the fore of Orestes' mind. Papo, his father, enjoyed relaxing in the late afternoon, lying on his bed and listening to his transistor radio on the bedside table. He was not tuned into the official state-controlled broadcasts, however. He always had the radio tuned in to a Miami station, where Cuban ex-pats gave their version of current events, particularly events in Cuba. Watching the official version on television and hearing a counter-narrative on the radio was a formative experience for Orestes, as he learned at a young age that there was more than one way to see and interpret what was going on. Where did the truth lie?

To this day, there is hardly anything that gets Orestes' dander up more than watching the news on Cuban television. With great animation he will tear the broadcaster's commentary to shreds, pointing out every fallacy, deconstructing every unfounded twist of logic, uncovering every bias. The running joke is that the daily news is always the same: everything good about Cuba (and its allies) and everything bad about the US (and its allies). He understands that the Radio Martí broadcasts from the dissenters in Miami is a mirror image of this kind of propaganda that passes for news. He longs, without much hope, for a day when the truth can be told from a variety of perspectives and people can weigh it all out in the balance, a day when what's shown and promoted on the news will have some coherence with the people's daily life experiences.

One of the most recent examples of his ranting at the tv came during the coverage of the shooting up of the Cuban embassy in Washington, D.C.

Among the many things he found appalling about the local reporting was the hypocrisy in the repeated commentary that the US had failed in its duty to protect the embassy. The history of the Peruvian incident in 1980 and the horrific events that followed is part of the yet untold truth that needs to be part of the public dialogue if reconciliation is ever to take place.

Regarding the events of 1980, young Orestes would be eye-witness to some of the horrors that occurred, not in the embassy itself, but in the aftermath of the occupation. A short time after the embassy episode, Fidel Castro struck a deal with Jimmy Carter, allowing for Cuban-Americans in Miami to come by boat to the Mariel harbor and retrieve any of their family members who made official application to emigrate. There had to be a stated motive for the wish to leave, and the most common reason given was, "I am a homosexual." LGBTQ persons at that time were not welcomed into the Revolution project; they did not fit the mold of the *hombre nuevo*, the new Revolutionary man (or woman). This did not mean that all these applicants were not straight, they just knew this declaration would give them a pass. The others who got a "pass," without even applying, were prisoners and psychiatric patients. So when folks from Miami came with their boats to pick up family members, they found they were required to take on other passengers as well, including these wards of the state who also did not fit the mold.

In between the time of the embassy occupation and the Mariel boat lift, Cuba experienced one of the darker episodes in its history. A massive hysteria of hostility against those who were leaving swept through the country. Presumably these were spontaneous uprisings of the people, aimed at showing their disapproval of those who were abandoning the country and casting their lot with the enemy. The so-called spontaneous nature of the events gave the government a convenient out for any culpability in the abuse. This deniability of involvement was hardly plausible, for as soon as a person would make application to leave, word somehow leaked out from the government offices into the neighborhoods and workplaces, and so-called "committees of repudiation" started forming. But whatever the root source, its victims, before getting to Mariel, had to endure mob-mentality aggression of the ugliest form. Three such episodes are etched into Orestes' memory.

Mr. Zamora was a fixture in the Pueblo Nuevo neighborhood, a good and noble man who loved engaging in conversations about anything having to do with sports. His family was well-known and well-liked; his brother Minini directed the rumba group Afro Cuba. Mr. Zamora was among those in the spring of 1980 who applied to leave Cuba and reunite with others of his family in Florida. Soon after he made application, the streets of Pueblo

Nuevo were filled with angry shouts of profanity. Young Orestes looked out his window to see a group of repudiators punching Mr. Zamora, shouting *gusano* (worm, the epithet of choice for emigrants of that period).

Orestes saw that one of the hostile horde had tied a bucket of rotting food scraps around the poor man's neck. Every few steps on the humiliating march down the street, someone would shout for him to show what garbage he was, and he was forced to reach in and get a handful of the composting mess and dump it on his own head; if he didn't comply he would receive another beating. Mr. Zamora made it to Miami, and those who have gone to visit him always remark about the world map on his wall. Just south of Florida, he has pasted a rectangular piece of paper over what was his country of origin. Two words are written on the paper: *No existe* (doesn't exist).

On another occasion, a family down the street was leaving, and when the repudiation committee came, Papo told Orestes to close the door and shut the shades on the windows. Orestes peeked out during the melee, and while he couldn't see the family, he did see the angry horde throwing eggs at the house, shouting profanities. Orestes remembers being so angry, telling his dad that he wanted to find a sack of rotten tomatoes to throw back at the crowd who was pelting the house with eggs. The third time he did not see the horror firsthand, but it filled his imagination. He heard the news about a little girl from his class at school who was going to leave with her family. Orestes remembers her as being pretty, sweet, and it broke his heart when he heard that a group of repudiators had gone to her house. He couldn't bear to imagine her being the brunt of such vile aggression. Childhood stories are often peopled by heroes and villains, and for a nine-year-old boy living on San Juan de Dios, it was pretty clear from these episodes who was who.

As it turns out, the Mariel emigrants were not received as heroes in Miami. The earlier waves of immigration after the Triumph of the Revolution had been mostly elite people, property and business owners. These were the ones who had quickly settled and adjusted and become leaders in the Miami community. The emigrants from the Mariel episode were hardly elite, and they met hostility and prejudice in their new promised land. Orestes remembers how they were recognized and profiled by their habits of fashion. During the 1980s in Cuba, those who were enamored with US culture loved to wear blue jeans. Their custom was to buy them a bit long and roll up the cuffs, to where a strip of socks would show. This was the hip fashion. It was not the style of the Miami elite, though, who would point and make fun of the Marielites whenever they saw them on the street sporting these high-water jeans.

Orestes says that if Papo had ever emigrated, he would not have suffered this profiling problem. His dad had other fashion challenges in the

Revolutionary culture. Papo had been brought up poor but proud, and the pride was demonstrated in his always wearing clean and ironed clothes, business style. The *hombre nuevo*, promoted in all the Revolution's propaganda, was a working man, and dressed accordingly, with work boots, khaki pants, and a t-shirt. If you dressed as Papo did, you were labeled bourgeois. Papo often lamented after hearing disparaging comments about his clothing, "I work in an office, not in the factory or the fields. What do I need with work boots?"

Papo and Esther's Pueblo Nuevo home in Orestes' childhood was grand central station for the neighborhood kids. What started out in his early years as a group of three—he and his buddies Edel and Bolo—grew into what would average twenty adolescent boys hanging around the house. Orestes' description sounds a lot like my own childhood home, which was also a place where kids gravitated. His dad, like mine, had set up a makeshift ping-pong table which created lots of competition and lots of stories. And I can see a lot of my mom in Esther, in her generous welcome and her desire to keep everybody well-fed. We have shared laughs about how some of our respective friends, years later, would come to visit, not so much to see Orestes or to see me, but to hang out with our moms and get a nostalgic taste of some of their comfort foods.

The growing group of teenagers developed their own fashion statements; they would have been called hippies if they had been living in the US. In Cuba, this subcultural group gained the label "freakies." Orestes and his buddies grew their hair long, did not follow the dress codes for the *hombre nuevo*, and spent a lot of time listening to and talking about rock and roll (and girls). The freakies did not go un-noticed by the Cuban police and security forces. Among the complicated legal code in the Revolutionary government, there was a set of regulations popularly referred to as the "danger laws." Under this law, anyone who looked like they might pose a danger to the Revolution, who looked suspect, could be arrested, as a crime prevention technique. If Fidel Castro or another high-profile leader was coming to or through town, the local authorities would execute the danger laws to get all the riff-raff off the streets, be they mentally ill beggars or prostitutes or freakies.

In his teenage years, Orestes and his friends were deemed dangerous on two occasions. Once, he and his friend Bolo, were picked up and hauled in for questioning. Bolo, in addition to his enthusiasm for rock and roll, had recently converted to Christianity, and invested a lot of passion and energy in learning about spirituality. As he and Orestes sat in the back seat of the police cruiser, Bolo found it to be a perfect opportunity to witness to the lost. He shared some of the gospel message with the officer, who responded with venomous vulgarity. The young evangelist was not dissuaded, telling the officer stories about how inspiring people like Saint Francis and Martin Luther King were. More profanity came back, saying that these were just freakies in another time, no good vagabonds. Finally Bolo said, "You can curse me all you want, but it doesn't bother me, because I love you." This didn't have the desired effect. The enraged cop thought he was getting hit on, and he turned around in the driver's seat and beat the hell out of Bolo. They arrived at the precinct, and the policeman ended the episode by shouting a few more profanities at them, and telling them to beat it.

Another experience involved a night in jail. This time, Edel and Orestes went to the park to hang out. Whenever they were on such an excursion, they would ask a friend as they got close to their destination, "How's the park?" The answer would either be "It's empty," (even though it might be full, this answer told them that none of their freaky friends were there), or "It's full," (even though it might be almost empty save for a small group of their pals). On this night, it was full, and they met up with Ivan Luis, better known as Beethoven, (the ring-leader of all things freaky in Matanzas), Papito, a few young women, and a young gay man with a long history of skirmishes with the police, who had not long been released from prison.

Without provocation, a policeman came up on his motorcycle and sidecar, and demanded the identity card from the gay teen. When the card was given, the officer looked at it and ordered the young man to walk to the precinct and meet him there. By this time, Edel, true to form, had already left with one of the women. The policeman then asked for Beethoven's, Papito's and Orestes' id cards. Beethoven and Papito surrendered theirs, but Orestes had not yet turned sixteen (the age when identity cards are issued), so he told the officer he was a minor. Presumably minors couldn't be arrested, so the protocol should have been for the officer to call Orestes' parents. But the officer squeezed him in the sidecar with Papito anyway, and with Beethoven on the back of the motorcycle, they headed off to the precinct.

When they arrived, a police detective was there to question them, first asking their names. "Orestes Roca Santana," then "Ivan Luis Rodriguez Monteja." Before getting to Papito, the officer looked the freaky leader up and down, and said, "Ivan Luis, aka Beethoven, right?" Beethoven affirmed the nickname, and the officer, continued, "Well, well, your reputation precedes you; you're known all the way to Lazo" (Esteban Lazo, at that time the Executive Secretary of the Communist Party in Matanzas, now the President of the Council of State and of the the National Assembly). "Hey, good for me, I guess," replied Beethoven. "Everybody wants to be famous."

Later on, the three of them would compare notes and observe that they never saw the gay youth anywhere in the precinct. They suspected that the police might have been using him as an informant, known in Cuba as a *chivato*. There are presumably chivatos on every block, in every church and workplace, but you never know for sure who they are. People who had spent time in prison were sometimes recruited to be snitches, under threat of doing more hard time.

The interrogation did not last long. It was late evening, and Orestes was placed in a drab, sparsely furnished room with only a red sofa and a television set. The officer who locked him in gave instructions not to touch anything or mess up anything, leaving him with this ominous warning: "Listen here you little shit-eater, when I come back, if I find the least little thing out of place, anything at all awry, I'm going to make you clean the entire room, including the floor, with nothing but your tongue." This threat made an impression on the not-yet-of-age freaky.

Some hours passed, and as darkness fell Orestes found that there was no light switch in the room. He tried turning on the tv, at least to shed some light, but it didn't work. In the pitch dark, he felt the urge to go the bathroom. He banged on the door and called for an officer, but no one came. More time passed, and the pressure on his bladder got stronger, until he finally couldn't hold it, and started urinating in the corner of the room. He forced himself to stop mid-stream when the nightmarish threat of the officer came back to his mind. He went back to the door and called out again; this time an older officer came and escorted him to the restroom. Orestes walked past the cells filled with various detainees, among them Beethoven and Papito, who gave him an encouraging shout-out as he passed.

In the meantime, Edel and his girlfriend of the night had gone back to the park and heard about what happened from some of the other young women who had witnessed it. He walked back to Orestes' house, half-expecting to find his friend already home with a story to tell; surely they wouldn't hold a minor in custody. He knocked on the door and asked Esther if Orestes was home. He wasn't. Edel knew he should tell her what had happened, but he was scared. He kept circling back to the house every thirty minutes or so to see if Orestes had made it home, but after a couple of hours he knew it was too late to keep the news a secret anymore. He screwed up his courage and filled Esther in on the situation.

With the rage of a mama bear Esther high-tailed it to the precinct to retrieve her first-born. She had no fear in filling the ears of every police officer in the precinct that night and as many government officials as she could find the next day. Papo had been out of the house when all this transpired, but by the time Orestes got home, he had heard and was awaiting his son, wanting to know every detail of the episode. He listened quietly, then shook his head, and said, "Well, son, now you've had your first taste of what it's like."

There's a lot that I have in common with Orestes, giving us a sort of separated at birth quality of friendship. Similar parents, hippy/freaky phases, love of all things rock and roll as well as religion. Of course, there are a lot of things we don't share in common. I never had to face the kind of harassment he suffered. Another difference in our experience is that all of my friends still live in the US, whereas in his case, he is the sole survivor. Virtually all of his circle of childhood and teenage friends have abandoned the *patria* to find a new fatherland. They are far flung, with some in the US, Canada, Spain, Portugal, Belgium, Germany, etc. Each has a story of their clash with Cuban society and their coming to a decision to go instead of stay.

The most unique story is Edel's, perhaps because he was the most nomadic, representing the ancient Abelite urge to stay on the move, while the rest pretty much traded in their Cuban Cain story for a different version of civilization. Edel and Orestes grew up together in Pueblo Nuevo. He was always intense, driven, maybe a little off-kilter, and he had no tact, no filters. He would say whatever was on his mind, no matter who was around, no matter the consequences. He was also obsessed from childhood with all things military; he idolized Che and Rambo. Growing up, he was hypercommunist, which was also a little strange in Orestes' group of friends.

His other obsession was women—*all* women—his attractions were not limited to the culturally prescribed preferences of body shape or skin tone. In their teenage years, they would often go out at night to hang out in Liberty Park. Edel lived down the street from Orestes and would swing by his house to get him, and they would take off. As soon as they got to the bridge, Edel would start using his pick-up lines, trying them out on every woman they passed—*every* woman—and if one happened to laugh or give him the time of day, Orestes knew he would be on his own the rest of the night.

As it happened, they were close enough in age that they both got the call to report in for military service on the same day. They went to the draft office to get their assignments: Orestes got to stay in Cuba while Edel was summarily sent off to Angola to join the war effort. That was fine for him; it gave him a chance to live out his Rambo fantasy. When Edel came back, though, he was different. Who knows if it was his experiences in the war that changed him, maybe PTSD, or if his affable zaniness just intensified while there. One thing was for sure: he was no longer the fanatic communist; his militance now found a home in the dissident camp. He was as blunt and tactless in his newfound dissent as he had been in his childhood pro-Revolution loyalty. His main goal was to find a way to get away.

Scheming his way out, Edel took a course in Havana to prepare him for work as a sailor on cargo ships. This would be his ticket to ride, and he didn't care where this ship took him. Sure enough, after completing the course he was placed on the crew of a ship taking goods to Canada, and his escape was in sight. But as fortune would have it, the Canadian customs found there was contraband tobacco on the ship and wouldn't allow it to dock, so he came back home. The next job was on a ship headed to Spain, and he boarded. This time they did make port, but there were other obstacles getting in the way of his plan. Edel knew that Cuban security agents were always hidden among the crew to thwart attempts at emigration, and he had a good idea who they were on this ship. A couple of the sailors seemed to always be lurking somewhere close to him, and he suspected they were there to keep vigilance and prevent him from bolting.

During some free time in the port city he and some of the crew, including these two, were hanging out, when Edel saw a bus pull up a block away. Without having planned anything out, he just took off, running at full speed. He leaped onto the bus and shouted for the driver to step on the gas; there were Cuban security agents chasing him. The driver obliged, and he was off to the races. Edel had a childhood friend who had emigrated to Asturias, and she had once invited him to come and visit her and her family if he was ever in Spain. So he asked the driver where he needed to go to get a bus to Asturias. The driver once again obliged, and next thing you know, Edel was knocking on his old friend's door. The invitation had been sincere, but limited to a short visit, and after several days, the husband of his friend showed him the door and sent him packing.

For a good while Edel lived on the street, working one odd job after another, and one of these jobs took him all around Europe. It was in some small town in Norway where another woman responded positively to one of his pick-up lines, and next thing you know, he was married, living the Norwegian life. This lasted a short while, but Edel was not one to be satisfied settling down with one woman, and when his wife found out about his extracurricular adventures, he was again told to hit the road. This pattern repeated itself several times, maybe four or five, until he landed another traveling job that took him to Scotland, which is where he lives now, with the latest of his wives, a university professor if you can believe it. He came back to Cuba not too long ago and visited Orestes, who found him to be the same old Edel. A ship with neither rudder nor anchor, whose response to the question "should I stay or should I go" is never complicated.

On one of our walks to Pueblo Nuevo, Orestes shared a random bit of trivia that he had read or seen on TV. "Whenever you are walking," he told me, "your body tends to go on auto-pilot; you don't really think about each step. And if you are in deep thought or conversation and have to step up onto a sidewalk or over a small pothole in the road, your body unconsciously gauges the distance and adjusts your pace, so that you don't take any awkward stutter steps; you stay in perfect stride." I theorized that such a phenomenon might be telling us something, maybe it's a subtle message that our bodies are elegantly designed to wander, to be on the march. We are *striders*, and these boots of Spanish leather are made for walking,

As Orestes saw first one and then another of his friends walking away from home to seek their fortunes elsewhere, he found himself on another adventure, a walk of faith. His conversion to Christianity, like that of Bolo, was filled with passion and a desire to learn. He came under the tutelage of several sages who helped guide his journey: his pastor Paco Rodés at the Baptist church, a charismatic Catholic priest named Padre Ramón, and Maestro Castellanos in the seminary. These mentors and others helped him discern his call to the pastorate, a role he has had at First Baptist Matanzas for nearly twenty years now. During these two decades, he has taken advantage of several opportunities to travel abroad, to Europe, Canada, the US. He has crossed paths again with some of his old friends. But he has always come back to Cuba, never taking advantage of any of the many opportunities to emigrate.

Recently, in one of our morning coffee conversations, I asked him why. What has been his thought process in deciding to stay in Matanzas, when all of his friends opted to go? I didn't expect his answer. First, silence. Then, "I don't know. No one has ever asked me that question, and I've never asked myself. I'd have to think about it." We sat with that for a few moments, and then he changed the subject and asked if I'd seen the movie *Of Gods and Men.* "No, but I've read about the story." The movie is based on a true story of a group of Christian monks in Algeria whose community was threatened by Islamic terrorists. They had befriended the local Islamic community (not terrorist), and the movie is about the monks' discernment process in whether to stay or to flee and find a safer place to live. Spoiler alert: They decided to stay, and they wound up getting killed.

I wonder now if Orestes really was changing the subject, or if there is something about this movie that gives a clue about his decision to stay. He is called to be pastor, to be shepherd, to a flock that sometimes has to drink not only still waters, but waters stagnated by decades of propaganda and half-truths. He is called to lead them to living waters. The grassy pastures may indeed be greener on the other side of the Cuban border, but the majority of his flock will never cross that border. So here he is, dealing with this calling and also struggling with the desire to fulfill a true shepherd's role (which involves being on the move) in an established institution (not easily moved).

In the institutional church, the traditional "pastor" role has tended to be more Caesar-like. No matter how democratic the governance structure, congregations, at least in Cuban church history, are heavily pastor-centered and expect their leader to be a good king, or at least a good manager. It's not surprising, given that the institutional church is a more a product of Cain's civilization project, not of Abel and his culture of wandering pastoral nomads.

The craziness of trying to navigate that inherent conflict of identity is in large part why Orestes asked me to join him on staff as second fiddle (his associate), to help simplify the work, lighten the administrative load, help shift the image and the infrastructure away from institution and more toward a movement. Our theme verse for the year-long process of dialogue and re-framing was a shepherd's call: "Enlarge your tents, and display your curtains, lengthen your cords and strengthen your stakes" (Isa 54:2). As we spent months in conversation parsing out the meaning of that verse for our community, coming to understand how bound up we were in institutional values, I could feel the blood of Abel rising up through the marble-tiled floor, giving the voice of a simpler and freer way at least a fighting chance. So now we find ourselves navigating our way through the craziness of competing stories. It's a start.

I suspect that given time for reflection, Orestes might come back to me with a clear answer as to why he is here, and I'm almost certain it will have something to do with the call to be a good shepherd for a flock under his watch care. In that respect, I also imagine that his answer would not be all that different than the answer Sila Reyna might give as to why she is in La Vallita. These two pastors, so opposite in so many ways, are in fact good friends, talking on the phone regularly, bearing one another's burdens, weeping together and rejoicing together through the tragedies and triumphs of the pastoral life. Their common bond is the Jesus story; they are both committed to this Way, a Way that can be followed just as well in Cuba as in Key West. You might even say that their story is not so dissimilar from the story of Jesus (other than the thousand and one contextual differences between Cuba and first-century Palestine).

Chapter 3

Walking with Alexis and His African Ancestors

Viajamos entre la tormenta, después de la explosión de Dios
Cada relámpago nos muestra fantasmagóricos de amor.[1]

—SILVIO RODRÍGUEZ, EXPEDICIÓN

Matanzas, Cuba
Sunday, March 25, 2018 CE
2:30 p.m.

The road toward friendship with Orestes Roca Santana was relatively smooth and easy; you might say the journey was likely and probable, maybe even predictable. It came naturally, given so many commonalities—family backgrounds, baptist identity, love for the Beatles. The same cannot be said for my journey to *amistad* with Alexis Morales O'Farrill. Ours is the unlikeliest and most improbable of relationships. Who could have predicted that a white Baptist hillbilly from the Blue Ridge mountains would be enjoying home-cooked meals prepared by a Santería priest and Abakuá member whose African roots run deep into the plains of Yoruba land? Crossing

---

1. Translated: "We travel through the storm, after the explosion of God. Every bolt of lightning shows us ghosts of love." Rodríguez, Silvio. "Expedición." *Expedición.* Fonomusic, 2002. Album.

paths with Alexis has required the farthest travel (culturally speaking), and it is a voyage that I am still navigating.

I met Alexis in 2016, via our common friend Lisbeth, who is like a daughter to Kim and me. At that time she was drumming and dancing in his Yoruba youth ensemble, Omó Ará (Children of the Earth), and she helped me arrange for Alexis and the group to offer presentations in Afro-Cuban folklore for visiting church groups. Then, sometime in the early spring of 2018, Alexis took a leap of faith and trust and invited Kim and me to join the group in their Sunday afternoon rehearsals. For about a year, we made the 1,385 step camino to the *Casa de Cultura* (community arts center) on the Calzada Tirry in Pueblo Nuevo. It's almost the same walk as we often make to get to Esther's, Orestes' mom. I find it interesting that Orestes and Alexis, close to the same age, grew up just a few blocks from each other, but were raised in largely different worlds.

Every city and town in Cuba has a *Casa de Cultura*, a centerpiece of the Revolution in its promotion of visual and performing arts for the community. In Matanzas, the Casa is named for hometown hero Bonifacio Byrne, an Afro-Cuban poet who was a major voice in the war for independence against Spain. Once that war ended, Byrne wrote eloquently and passionately against US intervention and control. So it is with a dose of humility twinged with historical shame that I always enter the building, and on those Sunday afternoons I would add not a small amount of dread to the other emotions I carried. I will jump ahead in the story to say that a couple of hours later, I would leave the building carrying a different set of emotions, pride and satisfaction at having survived, and gratitude to Alexis and his group for their generosity of spirit.

Back to the entrance, and the reason for dread: Once in the *Casa de Cultura*, we would climb the two flights of stairs to arrive at the performance studio, a seven hundred and fifty square foot, un-air-conditioned bare room with wooden floor and two large doorways opening up to balconies, creating at least the hope for a slight breeze to occasionally blow through the otherwise suffocating heat of the upstairs room in the eternal summer of Cuba. Here we would encounter Alexis, his life partner Milneris, and around a dozen or fifteen teens who have made the commitment to endure the grueling workout of Alexis' class for a solid eight hours each Sunday. Kim and I would generally make it through two.

During our two hours, I would take eight or ten of the longest steps of my life, over and over again, as Alexis would teach us the dance steps that accompanied a homage to one of the Orishas (the deities in the Lukumí popular religions). He would start the chanting, in a language completely unknown to me, and his students would know when it was their turn to respond. After enough repetition, I would sort of get the hang of the chant. Not so easy with the steps. If the African languages are completely foreign to me (not being in the family of romance languages that share some similar etymological foundations), then the rhythms are even farther afield. I would try my best to find a downbeat, to count to three or four to establish some pattern, but no, this was a different world. I finally learned that I had to quit trying, and just do my best to imitate what Alexis was doing.

He would line us up side by side in groups of six or seven, and would then get in front and start the step, with the far wall being our destination. Once each line reached the wall, we would turn around and head back to the other wall, again following Alexis. It would generally take about ten steps to get from one wall to the other, and watching Alexis, and watching his group of teens, I always would think to myself, "that looks so simple." Then I would try it, and discover that there are things that a body rooted in African culture can do that my body greatly resists doing.

Add to the rhythm challenge the movements of the neck and back and shoulders, the various subtle twists and turns that accompany each step, and now you might have an understanding where my weekly dread was coming from. At the end of two hours, I would generally have made it past the humiliating stage, and sometimes could even say that I was in step with the rest. Sometimes not, and sometimes I didn't get the chance, as Alexis would give me a pass—"Stan, sit this one out"—if it involved a somersault or some other move that might injure my less than pliable frame. I did get dizzy in one of the spinning steps and hit the floor with a thud, but fortunately, I sustained no injury to anything other than my pride.

To be fair, we weren't doing the steps for the full two hours. There was some warm up time, some stretching, some aerobics, maybe even a bit of salsa dancing, before getting into the heart of the practice. And there was always some teaching about the Orishas, giving some context for who it was we were paying homage to in our dancing and chanting. Several things always impressed me as a whole about this weekly experience. One was the commitment of these teens, devoting a full eight hours each Sunday afternoon/evening to the learning and formation. Some were preparing to apply to the national School of the Arts in Havana, which offers a major in Afro-Cuban folk art, including the dances and chants to the Orishas. Alexis has an impressive track record in getting students prepared for this highly selective and elite university. Others of the teens simply were there to learn and grow in their understanding and facility in practicing the cultural arts.

Another thing that impressed me was the quality of Alexis' teaching skills. He is a master instructor, and the ambience of that small and muggy room was always one of great respect, of the students for him and of him for his students. It was clear to me from the start that they were learning far more than dance moves. This was holistic learning, imbued with values and virtues and a commitment to lead a good and balanced life. This, I discovered, was the heart of Santería and the other branches of Afro-Cuban folk religions; they all involve the great balancing act of living in harmony with nature, with community, with oneself. It is a curriculum that served the hunting and gathering human species well for tens of millennia, before the dizzying onslaught of civilization and all of its imbalances.

Calabar, Nigeria
Sunday, March 3, 9,000 BCE
5:00 p.m.

Remember the story of Aganju and Yeyé Omo Eja, the primeval pair who left the Nigerian river valley to be fruitful and multiply and replenish the earth? As it turns out, they did not leave their native land *un-plenished.* The majority of the tribal peoples stayed and continued hunting and gathering and fishing in paradise, keeping a way of life intact for countless generations. But before there were story-tellers who could tell the tale of Aganju and Yeyé for generations to come, there had to be a genesis moment, a first story-teller, an initial meaning-maker if you will. The emergence of the Story was as epic an event in human history as that of leaving paradise to populate the rest of the earth.

It had to have happened sometime, at some precise moment in history, or pre-history to be more accurate. At some determined hour, (five o'clock in the afternoon is as good a guess as any), the universe went into contractions, and out of its labor pains, the gods were born, and with them came the Story. That's not to say that the divine didn't exist before this hour; it's just that this was the time when the deities came out of the dark womb of their pantheon and took shape in the human mind. Or, to be more accurate, they arose in a single human mind, for the Story had to start with somebody. This original Story-creator carried the name Al-Eje, "the axis," for he always seemed to be able to see the axis on which the wheels of any particular experience turned. Shift the axis, and transform the experience, he used to teach his tribe.

When Al-Eje was just a toddler, he was obsessed with numbers. He began counting, putting a number to everything—first there were fingers and toes, then teeth and ribs, and later it was how many breaths he took from sunup to breakfast, how many steps he took on his walks to the river, how many days between new moons, how many stars in the night sky. As he grew, he began to associate everything with a number. From these numbers he began to decipher messages and meanings, and then the numbers started sounding like music in his head, and the music morphed into visual art, and the art became theater, and the theater eventually turned into Story. As he reached the prime of life, the numbers and the music and the art and the drama and the Story all came together in his mind, and he called it Ifá. Ifá was a Rule. A Way. We might call it a cosmology, a science.

By the time Al-Eje reached old age, he had become convinced that the universe was more than meets the eye, that the gods inhabited a world larger than his, and he passed this conviction on to everyone within his own axis of influence. The realm of the gods was nine-fold, with four levels reaching down below the surface of the firm earth and sea bottom, and four levels reaching up to the stars and beyond, and a mid-level of space shared with the earth's creatures. Al-Eje found an axis of meaning when it occurred to him that everything that happens in the human world is but a resonant reflection of what is happening in those nine levels of divine interaction, above and below and alongside. The human story mirrors the story of the gods. He had long ago intuited that there is an energy to this interaction, something he called *aché,* a force that flows and animates and breathes through everything that exists. Living in harmony with *aché* signified for him that following the Ifá was not burdensome, but was a grace, an elegance.

But all that is getting ahead of the main Story, the epic event that happened on that Sunday afternoon, as the gestation period came to an end and a pregnant universe began giving birth to the gods. Al-Eje, whom we would consider an early adolescent at age twelve, had in fact just completed the traditional rite of passage into adulthood. The tribe's annual hunting and gathering journey began each year on the winter solstice, when they would leave the river valley and head southeast. Three moons later, they arrived at Calabar on the shores of the Atlantic ocean, where they would spend another three moons, before departing on summer solstice for the return trip through the Niger Delta and savannah plains before arriving at the starting point alongside the Cross River. This journey back took three moons, and then they spent three more in the river's lush valley before starting the pilgrimage all over again.

By the time Al-Eje turned twelve, he had spent years in preparation for the rite of passage, which consisted of this: He would be solely responsible for feeding his family for a full three months, from the day they left the Cross River until they reached Calabar at the Atlantic shore. He alone would do all of the hunting and gathering and fishing, and if he failed, his family would not eat. The rite of passage was serious business, not just for the adolescent, but for his entire clan. Tales were told of tribespeople having died from starvation along the route when a boy was not able to find adequate food, but no one was sure if this ever really happened, or if it was just a legend passed on to motivate the initiates to take their preparation work seriously.

The final ritual meal, signifying completion of the passage into adulthood, was the ocean catch on their arrival at the seashore. Al-Eje had provided well for the family for three months, and this meal was no exception. The family's celebratory banquet consisted of oysters, red snapper, and squid. After the mid-day feast, Al-Eje sat cross-legged for hours in the sand. His eyes became heavy, not only from a belly full of surf, but from counting sea shells and then grains of sand all afternoon. Losing count, he gave the sand a rest and started something easier, counting the waves that crashed onto the shore. In his increasing state of drowsiness, he got up to seven waves when, without warning, the undulating ocean transformed itself. It was suddenly not an "it" but a "she," a blue-clad being, with the multi-layered fabric of her skirts (he counted seven of them) rising and falling.

As the ocean goddess danced before young Al-Eje, the number seven kept repeating itself in the recesses of his mind, and in that liminal state between waking and sleeping, the number became music, and a single word formed the lyric of the song: *Yemayá*. It was the name of this Being that he understood to be a force beyond anything he had ever encountered. It was connected to nature, but was far more than a force of nature. It, or She, was the source of the ocean's massive and constant force. Neither Al-Eje nor any of his elders had up to that moment ever conceived of the concept of deity, or god, or goddess. Some months later, when he had experienced many more of these revelations, the word "Orisha" came to his mind as a title for these tremendous life forces. Something about this first Orisha that appeared, Yemayá, reminded him of his own mother, and he took it to mean that she was the mother of all. Al-Eje came to understand that she, like his own mother, was a force not to be taken lightly.

Neither was the fiery, virile, quick-tempered god who came to life another late afternoon on their journey back from the hunt, when Al-Eje was crouched down under a baobab tree, sheltering himself from a fierce storm. He was counting the seconds between the flash of lightning and the boom of thunder when the storm took shape as another Orisha. The formation came after a particularly impressive high voltage flash; his count had reached four when the deafening clap boomed like a drum, and in the ringing of his ears he heard a word: *Shango*. This was the force's name, the name for a god whose flashes and strikes and claps and booms cannot be predicted, and who is closely felt in the rhythm of the drums.

Throughout the remainder of that return trip, Al-Eje, who had now officially passed into adulthood, would witness the birth of many more Orishas. One that entered his mind while pondering a green and yellow field of grass and flowers was Orunmila. This was a god with whom Al-Eje would be in special relationship with for the rest of his life. Orunmila represented wisdom, knowledge of secret things, divination. It was he who gave the young man the wisdom to discern the axis on which the wheels of life turned. Then there was Obatalá, an inter-sex male and female deity adorned in all white, creator of the earth and its inhabitants, whose *aché* energy fostered all things compassionate, peaceful, and just in the world. Elegguá came to life when Al-Eje was skipping stones at the river. This Orisha emerged as a playful, childlike god, whose *aché* consisted of knowing when to open pathways and when to close them. He was especially useful on journeys. Ogún was born when Al-Eje was learning from his elders which of the flint stones make the best spear tips for hunting and which are better for fishing. Ogún's *aché* was in tool-making.

Toward the year's end, Al-Eje spent long days in the family's riverside tent, sitting by his dying grandfather's side. The tribal elder was suffering terrible pain from a disease that would much later be diagnosed as leprosy. It was on one of these days that the most impressive and enigmatic of the Orishas was born in the young man's mind. Babalú-Ayé emerged as a god unlike all the other gods. For while all the others bore some incredible gift or feat of strength, like our comic-book superheroes, this Orisha's *aché* was just the opposite: it manifested itself in weakness and suffering. Al-Eje watched in amazement as this deity appeared and assumed the pain of the old man. Leprosy did not leave the fragile body, but the pain did; it passed from suffering human to suffering god. The beloved grandfather would have three more days of life, spent in peace, grateful for the family he was leaving behind, grateful most of all for his grandson who had been midwife for so many gods to enter their world.

The young boy now turned young man would be the first of a long line of *babalawos*, something akin to priests, in the faith traditions of Africa that followed the emergence of the gods in human consciousness. Every generation that followed would have an Al-Eje in their midst, seeing messages in numbers and music and the drama and story of life, teaching the traditions of what in Cuba would come to be known as Santería, pointing out the axis on which the lives of both humans and gods revolved. I'm grateful that on the axis of my own revolution in the world I found myself spinning along with Alexis, one of those santeros[2] in Matanzas.

I once asked Alexis about his name, his second (maternal) last name, O'Farrill. "So you have Irish ancestry?" I asked. He laughed and said, "No, I'm 100 percent African, not a trace of Irish blood." He explained that his mother, Marta Rosa, was adopted by an O'Farrill. Her biological father, Moisés Zamora, was, in Alexis' words, a "complicated man," who had left his wife, Alexis' grandmother Rosa Amelia Montalvo, soon after their daughter was born. Mr. O'Farrill came into the picture soon after that departure, married the suddenly-single mom, and raised the infant girl as his own. So Marta Rosa gained her step-father's last name, O'Farrill, which is more than a bit ironic, given the history of the Irish coming to Cuba. Their venture came out of an intentional recruitment effort on the part of the sugar aristocracy to "whiten the workforce," having grown fearful that the growing population of enslaved Africans would one day find strength in numbers and revolt. Neither Marta Rosa O'Farrill nor her son Alexis had much to contribute to the whitening effort.

Alexis inherited his priestly gifts from his mother. The Afro-Cubans of Pueblo Nuevo actually considered her to be closer to the Orishas than the role of priest would imply. They almost deified her, due to her ability to offer wise counsel and her healing powers. I learned from Alexis that every family has its own special relationship, a resonance, with one of the Orishas, who becomes the family's patron deity. For the Morales-O'Farrill family, the resonance was with Babalú-Ayé, perhaps the most venerated of all the Orishas. What we know as *Santería* emerged when the arriving Africans found a way to maintain their faith practice by concealing each of their deities within a Catholic saint or other Christian figure, and Babalú-Ayé found his hiding place behind the biblical figure of Lazarus, the poor beggar outside the gate of the rich man, with a dog licking the boils that covered his body. One of the most common figurines found in Cuban homes is this parabolic saint, on crutches, with a Dalmatian at his side.

Babalú-Ayé always makes me think of my childhood, when I often sang a chant in his honor (without having a clue what I was doing). I explained this to Alexis after asking him a question I've asked many Cubans: "Have you ever heard of Ricky Ricardo?" He gave me the same answer I almost always get here: "No." (There was one exception—a museum curator in Cienfuegos actually knew the history of Desi Arnaz). I shared with Alexis my memory of having a toy set of bongos, playing along with Ricky when

2. A santera or santero is a priestess or priest in the Afro-Cuban religions. The title comes from the manner in which the enslaved peoples disguised their religious practices, by connecting ancestor worship to the veneration of the saints.

he was at his nightclub (or little Ricky when he came along), belting out *Babalú* with great intensity. Some time back I watched a re-run of one of these episodes, and cringed when I saw a bit-actor clad in stereotypical African native costume run out onto the stage and jump around wildly during Ricky Ricardo's chant. It made me grateful that the *I Love Lucy* phenomenon completely bypassed Alexis and most other Cubans.

On the more serious side, I never fail to be deeply moved whenever Omó Ará's dance/chant presentation of the Orishas gets around to San Lázaro/Babalú-Ayé, which they always save for near the end of the program. The way the young people portray the deity who suffers is incredibly poignant, almost painful to watch, as the dancers embody tremendous agony before transitioning to a beautiful movement of healing.

Alexis' ancestors made the middle passage from Nigeria to the New World, and then made their third passage when they were driven like livestock to the auction block in the municipality of Jagüey Grande. There they were forced to work in the sugar cane fields of the Matanzas province. In the Nigerian religious tradition, not only each family but each pueblo would have a patron Orisha to guide their lives and grant them a particular kind of energy. For his ancestors who settled in Toriente, a small village which is part of Jagüey Grande, the local deity was the same as his family's, Babalú-Ayé, whom they safely concealed behind the figure of San Lázaro in order to maintain their faith practice under the vigilance of Catholic overlords. To this day, the village of Toriente is associated with the compassionate and healing energy of San Lázaro. Alexis regularly travels back there, not only to re-connect with family, but to participate in the various rituals dedicated to the wounded-healer god.

Alexis also taught me that while every family and every village or town has its particular relationship with one of the Orishas, every individual is also "wired" to find his or her own personal attachment to one of the sacred forces. Alexis discovered early in life that he is connected to Elegguá, the mischievous, child-like deity who is responsible for opening pathways, or closing them as the case may be. This Orisha, then, is the god of movement, of travel, blessing the way.

Alexis tells me that from his childhood, he had people coming to him seeking a blessing for a trip they were taking. So when he arrived at late adolescence and it came time for him to go through the ritual discovery of his personal Orisha, it was no surprise to anyone that he was "seated" with Elegguá. He has this Orisha's heart, and he has Elegguá's smile. Alexis surely embodies the playfulness of Elegguá; we found that out in his Sunday afternoon classes. He could be a strict taskmaster for getting the steps of a dance right, but he always tempered the hard work by provoking raucous laughter.

It is also no surprise, given his affinity for Elegguá, that Alexis himself is a world traveler. He has taken multiple trips to Mexico and Canada, and has also traveled throughout South America, Europe, and Asia. He remembers well his first time traveling outside of Cuba; it was to an international folk festival in Quebec. "Folklore" is how people in Cuba now describe the Afro-Cuban religions and cultural practices. While some might hear this as a demeaning expression, trivializing the tradition and robbing it of its genuine power, Alexis has no problem with the term. At its root, the word "folklore" means "the people's learning," and for him, it speaks to the millennia-old oral traditions that connect people to their earliest roots.

He was surprised to discover the universality of this connection on his first trip to Canada, where one hundred and twenty-one countries were represented at the folk festival, each offering presentations of their own particular brand of folklore. Alexis found that his own Nigerian-based drumming and dancing and chanting reverberated with that of presenters from many other countries. He especially remembers the connections he made with a group of elderly white men from Croatia, all sporting long gray beards, who resonated deeply with his homage to the Afro-Cuban Orishas. Alexis learned that the sacred energies were not limited to the Lukumí tribes of Nigeria and their descendants. The music and the movements might have been born there, but had over the course of history spread throughout the globe as the original travelers got the blessing from Elegguá to venture out in every direction, from Croatia to Canada.

Matanzas
Tuesday, August 20, 2019 CE
4:30 p.m.

I was in our apartment at the Kairos Center on that hot Tuesday afternoon, getting ready to go over to Orestes' and Wanda's to help with dinner prep, when the Center receptionist gave me a shout, *eStán!* (The Cuban way of pronouncing my name). *El profe está aquí para verte.* The professor is here to see you. *El profe.* That's what the Kairos Center folks respectfully call Alexis. I descended the two flights of stairs down to the lobby and was greeted with a broad smile. We went through the Cuban salutation ritual of "how's the family?" I gave him the latest news of how the North Carolina folks were doing, and he gave me an update on how his two sons are faring—they, like their father, are world travelers, teaching and performing Cuban folklore. Eddie, the elder son, is in Russia, while Joseito, the younger, is in Italy. Alexis once told me that Eddie is more like him when it comes to the "should I stay or should I go" dynamic. He loves to travel, but always has his eye set on returning home. José, by contrast, left Cuba for good and is establishing his roots in Italian soil.

The *profe* was holding a *jaba*, that is, a shopping bag, full of something, and I knew I was in for a treat. He had gone to visit family in Jagüey over the weekend, and was here to share some of the treasures he had brought back. The bag was filled with boniatos (sweet potatoes), okra, and plátanos (the cooking variety). He seemed to be in a bit of a hurry, so we didn't have time to talk. If we had, I would have shared with him my irritation and complaints about something I had read earlier in the afternoon. I had made the 216-step walk to Liberty Park after lunch, to connect to the wifi and catch up on emails. Someone on Facebook had posted the link to a *New York Times* series that had just started, "Project 1619." As I read the intro, it was apparent that the journalists on this project had not consulted with Alexis Morales O'Farrill or any other Afro-Cubans.

The project claims to commemorate the four hundredth anniversary of when enslaved Africans first set foot "on American soil" in August of 1619. *A-ah-ahh-ah!!! That's not right!!!* It's yet another example of not realizing that the US does not constitute the whole of America. The *Americas* include many countries, including Cuba. While Alexis is not like Alex Haley (he cannot point to a Kunta Kinte figure as his first ancestor to set foot on "American soil"), he does have roots. He traces them, at least spiritually speaking, back to the first enslaved Africans who made the middle passage and landed in the Matanzas Bay. Contrary to the *New York Times*, this first instance of human trafficking on American soil occurred in 1517, more than a full century before a similar ship would land at Jamestown.

Alexis' ancestors were not the first Africans in the New World (a small number had arrived in Española in 1502), but his were the first in what would become the trans-Atlantic slave trade. They made the journey from the Old World shores of Calabar, Nigeria, without having had the benefit of struggling with the age-old question: "should I stay or should I go?" They were not given the choice; these unfortunate souls had been captured in inter-tribal warfare and compelled to march to the Calabar coast (the "first passage"), where they were forced aboard a slave ship. The *Times* journalists missed a good story, "Project 1517," we might call it. The sad saga involved the most ironic and tragic connections between Christianity and the conquest of the new world, as that first slave ship's journey had its genesis in a well-intentioned but poorly thought out idea of one of the most progressive and liberal minds of the day, Bartólome de las Casas.

Las Casas had come to Cuba fifteen years earlier, under the same terms as many of his Spanish compatriots. He was given an *encomienda*, a land grant that included a group of enslaved Taínos at his command. The land was located, appropriately enough for the irony of this story, in a region called *Sancti Spíritus*, Holy Spirit. The "spiritual" justification for encomienda slavery was that it was the means for good Christians to evangelize and convert the savage lost souls to the faith, and at the same time teach them the values of hard work. Las Casas, a Dominican priest, was soon converted to a more enlightened way of thinking through the preaching of one of his fellow Dominicans, Antonin Montesino.

After his conversion, the newly liberalized priest came to lament the cruel treatment of the enslaved Taíno people; he emancipated those from his encomienda and became a champion for the human rights and humane treatment of all indigenous people. Because of his decades-long commitment to this cause and his sophisticated reasoning in laying out the basis for his argument, Las Casas has been called the father of the modern notion of human rights. In contemporary conversations in Cuba, the legacy of the Dominican friar can be heard in a question posed whenever someone is acting in a particularly tender way toward another: "Who do you think you are, Padre Las Casas?"

It was in 1517 that a not-so-bright idea occurred to Father Bartólome. He was witnessing the Taíno people suffer and die from exhaustion due to the overwork and torturous overseeing in the mines and fields, and he felt helpless to change their plight. One day he was thinking about his childhood in Seville, and he remembered interacting with enslaved African who were integrated into the work force there in his home town. He reasoned: what if he could convince the Spanish royalty to ship down a few hundred African slaves to share in the toil of the mines and cane fields? Maybe, just maybe, the extra hands would lighten the load and keep the Taíno from being worked to death.

Bartolome de las Casas traveled to Spain early in 1517 for the express purpose of making his appeal. His meetings with the ruling class was ultimately successful; later that year the first slave ship sailed for the Americas. Toward the end of his life, Las Casas, who for six decades had spoken and published widely on the necessity for ensuring human rights, confessed to the now obvious foolishness, if not utter stupidity, of his idea. He had not foreseen the resulting catastrophe: bringing a few hundred Africans to ease the burden of a dying race of Taíno soon morphed into the horrific project of trans-Atlantic trafficking and the cruelty of plantation slavery.

I asked Alexis about this part of his history, how the Orishas figured into the slave trade. How could the gods have allowed African culture, steeped as it was in the Lukumí virtues of balance and harmony, to descend into the non-virtuous practice of slave trading? I could understand, if totally disagree with, how the Europeans would find justification for their involvement. If you're looking for it, there's plenty of precedent in the Judeo-Christian scriptures to inspire the idea that some humans have divine permission to conquer and enslave others (just as you can find precedent for movements to eradicate such practices). But what was it that gave rise to such a horrific idea within African society? Alexis' answers were not far afield from what I might have heard had I been sitting at the feet of another Al-Eje, a babalawo from eons past, who taught and practiced the faith at the very time when the idea of slavery was in fact born in the human mind.

Cross River Valley, Nigeria
Sunday, August 3, 8,000 BCE
2:00 p.m.

Before heading to the grove of baobab trees, under whose shade he would continue the training of his young babalawo apprentices, Al-Eje consulted the Ifá (that his ancestral namesake had developed), knowing that some strange winds were blowing through his tribe. He had no way of knowing that the same winds were blowing through the Fertile Crescent's Palestinian tribes, and within a few short millennia would blow through up-to-now nomadic hunting and gathering cultures around the globe, including the Yamna in Green Spain, the Inca in Peru, the Maya in Guatemala and southern Mexico, and the Taíno in the Caribbean islands. What he did know was that something strange was filling the hearts and minds of some of his tribespeople with troubling thoughts, thoughts of giving up the annual march to the coast and back, thoughts of plowing land and cultivating crops instead of reaping what they had not sown, thoughts of a more settled life, of building barns to store the surplus of their bountiful yields, thoughts of constructing villages and towns and cities and empires, complete with kings who would not only exercise control over new civilizations, but would conquer all those who got in their way as they expanded in every direction.

Some of Al-Eje's students had been caught up in these winds, or waves, while others had encountered friends or family members who had felt them. As it was something new, never before experienced, they were confused, and had gone to their instructor to ask what was happening in the world. It felt like the wheels of the world were spinning off its axis. Al-Eje listened to their disquiet, and not having answers, went to consult with the oracle. He then spent three days in solitude with the Ifá, deciphering numbers that slowly became music and then story and then drama in his mind. Only then, when the vision was clear, did he call for his students to gather around him.

"The world," he explained to them, "seems to us to be fixed; the cosmos appears to be stable, steady, static. Does not the ground feel firm? Does not the sky appear to be as it always has been? Have we not always relied on and trusted in its constancy? But I have learned that this is not how the world is at all." Al-Eje explained the truth this way: "The world, like each of us, is moving. The entire cosmos is like a pilgrim, always on the march, just like we are on the march, headed to an unknown destination. We may not be able to feel it, but the Orishas know it: four levels below us, the rocks that burn in the deepest places are stirring, clashing. And we may not be able to see it, but the clusters of stars four levels above us at the world's rim are stretching outward." It would be another ten thousand years before practitioners of another faith tradition, the science of physics, would consult the numbers of their oracle and explain to the world the drama of our ever-expanding universe.

At this point in his instruction the students looked up at the sky to see if they could catch a glimpse of this cosmic pilgrim march. Al-Eje shifted metaphors. "You can think of it this way: The world is like a river, forever flowing. Consider the Cross River that we know so well. We have followed its path, and have seen that when its banks are wide, the river's currents move silently, in tranquility, with deep pools underneath, so that you hardly see any movement. Then, you round a bend in the river, and see that the banks have closed in, squeezing the river into a narrow path. The water suddenly becomes turbulent, with strengthened currents crashing over rocks. It is dangerous, difficult to navigate.

"Then, the river bends again, and suddenly the banks expand once again, and the waters return to their peaceful flow. For as long as our ancestors have told us stories, stories that go back to the beginning of time, the river of our world has had wide banks, and the currents have flowed peacefully. We have been living in the deep pools of time, hunting and gathering, making our marches to the sea and back, year in and year out, living in peace with other tribes who are making their way through the world.

"But now I have seen that the river recently made a turn, and the banks of the world have closed in. Life is going to get more and more turbulent, dangerous, difficult to navigate. The Ifá did not reveal how long this passage of the river will last. It may be longer than any of us can imagine. And in this time of troubled waters, the Orishas, like us, are having to adjust to the changing flow; they are learning, just as we will have to learn, how to navigate. We have never known these kinds of troubled times before, but we do know what it is like to feel pressure, to be squeezed in by fear, like we do when a pack of wolves emerges, hungry for the meat of our sheep. We know that these kinds of crises sometimes bring out the best in us, and sometimes they reveal our flaws. From what I understand of the Ifá's message, the changes we are seeing in people around us, these strange new desires, are expressions of the pressure and fear that the turbulent flow of the world is creating. We will wait and see whether those fears bring out the best in us, or reveal our flaws. I suspect they we will experience both.

"We have always understood that the Orishas are not perfect. They have their flaws, too, just as we have our defects. We have always accepted that as a part of life. So when the life forces of the Orishas flow through these narrow and dangerous passes, they will not always know how to act out of their virtues. We are connected to them, so be prepared: we will not always know how to act, either. There will be violence. There will be deception. Our relationships will not always be just and good. But we are to trust in the aché of our Orishas, even with their flaws, for they will grow, as the world is growing. They will learn to navigate the turbulence and act with virtue, and in so doing, so will we, through our connections with them."

Al-Eje went on to explain some of the specifics of what the oracle had revealed to him in his time of discernment and visioning. The tribes would slowly change; the hunting and gathering of small tribes would give way to life in larger, more dense clusters, in settlements they would call cities. These cities would not be like the mobile tent villages the tribes were accustomed to; they would be anchored in place to one piece of earth. Life in the anchored cities would be complicated. The Ifá also revealed that fear would overtake trust in the cities. A fear-based life would lead to many completely new and completely disagreeable things, such as warfare and conquest and slavery (Al-Eje went to great pains to explain what these new concepts, these futuristic phenomena that the numbers had communicated to him, signified).

"But take courage," he told them. He had also learned from the Ifá that the only way to overcome the horrors would be to stay as closely connected as possible to the Orishas. Each family would need to be tightly woven into the life force of their family Orisha. Each individual would have to be as tightly connected as possible to the energy of his or her patron Orisha. They trusted that the Orishas would grow; they would learn. They would develop wisdom to overcome confusion and courage to overwhelm fear. They would develop passion for peace and justice to overpower the tendency to war and slavery.

In the meantime, Al-Eje learned, (and it will be a *mean* time, he suspected), the flaws of the gods will be transformed into exquisite and mesmerizing music. Without the narrowing of the banks, the world might never know the music, the dance, that would be forged in the fires of the river's dangerous flow. The Ifá's numbers had morphed in Al-Eje's mind into music that he could neither replicate nor explain: Cuba's rumba, Brazil's bossa, the Mississippi Delta's blues. "None of this will come about," he intuited, "if the river stays in its calm flow. A day will come when the world once again rounds a bend to experience peaceful waters, with deep pools of tranquility, but when that day comes, there will be so many beautiful things in the currents that one might not recognize it as the same river." As Al-Eje's students looked on and listened with confused and wondrous looks, he came back time and again to the main point he had gained from the Ifá: "Sink deeply into your Orisha's energy. Live in constant connection to that aché. It's the only way to navigate the turbulence."

Matanzas, Cuba
Tuesday, October 20, 2020 CE
1:00 p.m.

I was able to ask Alexis this question, about the rise of slavery and the role of the Orishas, when he came by the Kairos Center early one afternoon, just to talk. It was a national holiday, Cuban Culture day, so we chatted some about music, but he let me know that this was the eve of a more important day for him. The next day, October 21, would mark the thirty-seventh anniversary of his initiation as a *Santo*. He had gone through the ceremony of being "seated" with his Orisha (Elegguá) and had entered what is the equivalent of Christian priesthood when he was but thirteen years old.

Alexis also spent time in the conversation telling stories about his mother. I had asked him what he was going to do to celebrate the anniversary, and his eyes became moist as he said he wasn't going to do much, maybe light a candle, but that mostly it would be a day to remember the influence and impact of his mother, who passed away four years ago. As he began telling me stories about her, I began to feel a similar nostalgia for my own mother, as there seemed to be some connections of spirit between these two women who had lived in very different worlds. A prime connection was their insistence on making sure everyone who came into the realm of their abode got a plate of food. Both women spent a lot of time in the kitchen. And both suffered and died from cancer, enduring the suffering in heroic ways.

We shared some of our "mama's cooking" stories, and I promised him that some day soon I would bring him a sample of my attempts to replicate the southern cuisine of my mom's kitchen. To his delight, that day came just two days later, when I showed up at his door with some boniato pie, not overly sweet, as he is diabetic. More stories spilled out, and at some point I reminded him that we hadn't really delved into the question I had raised about the emergence of slavery, and the role of the Orishas. He was happy to switch gears and enter into professor mode; he is a passionate teacher of African religious tradition.

He first said that many people focus on the role of the Europeans in the slave trade, the culpability of the conquistadors in the human trafficking that brought Africans to the New World. But of course, it wasn't just the Portuguese and Spanish who were in the trade. The African empires were complicit, capturing for the most part prisoners of war and selling them to the Europeans to ship across the Atlantic. How and why did this phenomenon emerge in Africa? "Simple," he told me. "Through the development of civilization." He explained that as some tribes developed more complex societies based in a more sedentary, established, urban life, the development was accompanied by the urge to expand and enrich their realms. This meant they began waging wars on other, less developed, more traditional tribes, and these wars gave birth to the concept and practice of enslavement.

"There's an important lesson to learn here," Alexis told me. "There is a balance in life, a balance between goods and ills. They accompany each other. The more extreme and ample the goods, the more extreme and ample the ills." I listened to him describe the irony of history, how it was the very sophistication of the civilized tribes that made possible the most horrific of human ills, such as that of war and slavery. "We were better off before," he said, referring to the pre-civilized, nomadic tribal life.

He then segued back to stories of his mom, who, he said, was deeply connected to the old, indigenous wisdom of the African religions. He lamented how in modern times, especially in tourist destinations like Cuba, the religions have become something of a show. Many of the practitioners play to their audience, giving what they think the crowd wants, in terms of not only the music and dance, but in practices like animal sacrifice in healing rituals and other ceremonies that pay tribute to the Orishas. Alexis said that if you are a true healer, what is important is your *faith*, your *intention*, and it isn't necessary to cause suffering among animals to practice your gift. His mother had always said that there were more than enough healing properties in a simple glass of water, with intention and faith, to achieve most anything.

Alexis then explained that in the indigenous African practices, the animals who were slain in tribute to an Orisha were cooked and and the meat was shared among the community. It was basically a way of sharing a feast for both your community and the Orishas to enjoy. It had nothing to do with appeasing a god. It was only a few days earlier that I had heard something very similar from a friend who was studying the book of Leviticus, and had discovered that the earliest Jewish rituals of animal sacrifice were just the same, feasts in which the people enjoyed the meat and God enjoyed the aroma of the smoke. It was much later in the history when the concept of sacrifice for atonement of sin came into the faith tradition.

"And how about the role of the Orishas?" I asked. If everything that happens in the human world is somehow reflecting what is happening in the world of the deities, what was going on in that divine world during the emergence of slavery? "Yes," he said, "that's a great question, and to answer it, you first have to understand something very important that distinguishes African religions from other world religions. And this is not to critique other religions—we have the greatest respect for Christianity. Jesus is an imminent example of God at work in the world; I love going to mass and participating in the liturgy. I am a believer! But here is what African tradition has to offer: the gods are not perfect. They have their defects, their flaws. They are neither omniscient nor omnipotent. They live, as we do, with the balance of good and ill. So the beauty of civilization brought on the ugliness of slavery which then brought on the beauty of resistance and work for justice. The deities are working it out, as we are, in a world that is constantly changing.

"But you know something else?" He asked. "It's not just that the gods share in our human struggles. It's that they share themselves with us, or better, we embody their traits, their very presence. When I went through the ceremony of being seated with Elegguá, it was simply a confirmation of something that had been there all along, the divinity within me. And you have it too! Yes!" (His emphatic confirmation was in response to my disbelieving look). "I remember years ago when you were guiding a group of US civil rights leaders, and Omo Ará offered them a presentation. Then we were able to interact with these giants of history, these heroes who had shed blood for the cause of justice and human dignity. You brought us together with them—and what a gift that was to us! You have no idea how much we needed that infusion of spirit at the time." He was right, I only remembered how much of an impact his group had made on the civil rights leaders.

"And then, sometime later, you were guiding and translating for an interfaith group comprised of Muslims and Christians and Jews, and they, too, came to our performance and interacted with us. After you and the group left, we spent three hours talking about it! We were amazed that you were there translating the experiences of four different worlds—the Lukumí, the Muslim, the Christian, and the Jewish—who would have imagined that happening? It was then that your own divinity came through so clearly to us. *Yes,* the divine is seated with you, too, it doesn't matter whether you've been through the seating ceremony or not."

I almost burst out laughing at this declaration, not only at my extreme discomfort at receiving such a profound blessing, but at how that particular experience with the interfaith group was a confirmation of Alexis' teaching about the balance between good and evil. While there were many good and beautiful spirits within that interfaith group, the leadership of the group (who happened to be Christian), turned out to be the worst example of the "ugly American syndrome" I've ever seen, disrespectful of the Cubans and Cuban culture on every turn, constantly complaining. In their evaluation of my work, they accused me of, among other things, not giving them any experiences of interacting with black Cubans.

All this, which I hadn't thought about in a long time, flooded back to my mind as I looked at Alexis, appreciating the blackness of his face, a photo of which had provided such a simple refutation of their accusation. He didn't know any of this, and I was tempted to launch into the whole sordid story with him. But the present look on his face, reflecting his pure joy at remembering the encounter, was something I didn't want to ruin. Sometimes joy does not need to be balanced with anger and resentment.

Instead, I found a way out of the discomfort with my divinity by turning the conversation back to pie and to our mothers' cooking. I now realize, after hearing Alexis talk about the divinity residing within humanity, that I erroneously wrote earlier in this chapter that his community of Pueblo Nuevo had "almost" deified his mother, due to her spiritual giftedness and wisdom. There was no "almost" about it, she was definitely considered divinity in the flesh. It caused me to reflect on the way my mom was "created in the image of God." Are our beliefs so different at their core? I know that millennia of institutional and credal development have caused believers of different religious traditions to appear separated on the surface, but could it be that in the subterranean strata, the roots of our indigenous pre-civilized faiths are all connected?

Maybe sometime I'll get Alexis to do some discernment work with me and see which of the African Orishas is rolling along on the axis of my life. I still have some doubts to work through before any seating ceremony will ever happen. Alexis, though, had no doubts about his own resonance with Elegguá, the opener and closer of paths. Kim and I are a couple of months away from having our current visa expire. All of our paperwork is in for the application for another year's stay. We sure could use Elegguá's blessing. As my contemporary Al-Eje and I ended our talk of pie and mothers and Orishas and slavery and human divinity, I asked him if he would sing the tribute chant to Elegguá, and he gladly obliged. Though I have no idea what the words mean, I'm going to carry the chant with me as a prayer for the next couple of months.

Para suayo omo nia laguana
Para suayo mamakenediabo-eh

Chapter 4

Walking with Lázaro and His Dutch Ancestors

Yo no sé lo que es el destino;
caminando fui lo que fui.[1]

—SILVIO RODRÍGUEZ, EL NECIO

While the African and Spanish roots of *cubanía* are hard to miss when walking through Matanzas, or any other Cuban city, there are other ingredients, not-so-obvious, that flavor the culture. For instance, one doesn't generally think of Holland when eating pork in a paladar or dancing the meringue in a Cuban nightclub, but the Dutch influence has its place in the mix. It began at the dawn of the seventeenth century as the various European powers set sail for Cuba, vying for control of the island and its vast resources, and the influence continues to the present day (I'm reminded of this quite often when working at the Kairos Center, as one of their primary sources of funding comes from *Kerk in Actie*, a faith-based foundation in Holland).

A brief clarification: While this chapter deals with the arrival of the Dutch in Cuba, and in particular the influence this part of the world has had and continues to have in Matanzas, I do not personally know any Cubans who trace their lineage to the Netherlands. The main character of the

---

1. Translated: "I don't know what the destiny is; walking, I was what I was." Rodríguez, Silvio. "El necio." *Silvio.* Ojalá, 1992. Album.

chapter, Lázaro Ceballos, is not aware of any ancestry hailing from Holland. That said, with his pale skin tone and light brown hair, it is not far-fetched to think that *Ancestry.com* would reveal some percentage of his blood line being connected to wanderers who at some point in the distant past migrated from the Low Countries. I chose Lázaro to be the protagonist of this particular ingredient in the mix of Cuban culture for a couple of reasons: one, there is definitely a spiritual connection, seen in his fascination with Flemish mysticism of the Middle Ages. Then there is the artistic connection, with Van Gogh serving as one of the prime sources of inspiration for his artistic work. As a bonus, Lázaro's one adventure outside of Cuba involved a trip to Holland a few years back. Here is his story.

Matanzas, Cuba
Wednesday, October 7, 2020 CE
7:00 p.m.

It is a weekly Wednesday ritual. Kim and and I make the two thousand two hundred and thirty-seven step walk to the Versalles neighborhood home of Lázaro Ceballos and Tamara Caballero to have dinner with them and their teenage genius of a daughter, Yeni María. A few years back, the dinner would have included the presence of their twenty-something son, Lazarito, but last year he made the decision to leave the patria; he and his young bride are seeking a better future in Brazil. Lazarito's unexpected departure, something of an emotional tsunami for the family, created what for me was an unexpected change in the family dynamics. They have always been one of the most deeply connected families I have ever known (outside of my own), and until a year ago, they were a paradigm of simplicity; with zero interest in the internet and all its bells and whistles. But now they are "connected" in the modern sense: they quickly entered the world of cell phones and apps so that they can have daily video chats with the Brazilian member of the family. It helps to have Yeni María close by; I suspect that Cuba's teenagers are serving as the in-house IT staff for many families across the island.

To get to Versalles Kim and I have to cross the Yumuri River, and there are several routes and bridges from which to choose. Kim prefers crossing at the Concordia Bridge, where there is a good view of the Matanzas Bay. This deep bay provides a depth of spiritual resource for her, so that simply walking close to it restores her soul. For me, the same can be said of crossing the threshold into Lázaro's house; it is a wellspring of sacred energy. I'm not the only one who feels this. Many times we have taken small groups of visitors there to experience a house prayer meeting, and I don't know how many people have later commented that they felt something palpable and deep when they walked into the home. The prayer meeting was simply a means of putting into more formal expression what was already there in the atmosphere of the humble dwelling.

Lázaro is many things to many people: he has made his living for years as a painter (icons being his current passion) and potter, but he is also a prison chaplain, musician and composer. Add to that a long history of work as a martial arts expert (aikido). While I appreciate all of these roles, he is something else to me: he is my spiritual director, even though I have never asked him to be and he never offered. It just happens. Lázaro knows how to listen. He knows when to be silent, and he knows when to respond.

More often than not, his responses surprise me, like the time I was reeling emotionally from being guide to an interfaith group (the same one Alexis recalled), an experience that turned out to be the most difficult and draining of my time in Cuba. I was feeling deeply depressed, and described the situation to him. I confessed that my spiritual resources simply were not adequate for meeting this particular challenge.

I suppose I was hoping for some sympathy, so was more than a bit taken aback when he responded with a huge smile and responded enthusiastically, "That's great! Time to discover new resources!"

"What?" I asked. He explained, "Experiences like this are to be cherished; they come to us as gifts! It's important to discover the limits of your resources; without experiences like these that bring us to our wits' end, we will stay in the shallow end of the pool. But coming to the limit pushes you to dive deeper, dig deeper, because there are more resources available for you to discover." Part of me wanted to scowl, but the better part of me wanted to laugh, which I did, and I soon set out on the diving/digging expedition.

Another surprise happened on this particular Wednesday evening over dinner. I thought I had made a great discovery and was excited to share it with Lázaro, sure that he would appreciate it. I had been doing some reading on spirituality and stumbled across a name I had never heard in all my years of reading church history. Knowing that Lázaro is a faithful disciple of the fifteenth-century Spanish mystic San Juan de la Cruz (Saint John of the Cross), I knew he would be interested to learn about a lesser-known mystic who had lived a century earlier and had been one of the primary influences on San Juan. I started telling him the story of my reading, how I had found a name I had never heard of, a medieval mystic who had written a lot about the contemplative life, a Flemish monk named Jan—

Lázaro's face brightened as he finished my sentence with enthusiasm: "Ruysbroek!"

"*What?* You've heard of him? I took a class in seminary on the history of contemplative spirituality and his name never came up."

"Yes, he's phenomenal. When I got so deeply immersed in the writings of John of the Cross, I wanted to go back and see who were his founts of inspiration. Let me show you. . . " With this he darted out of the room and came back with a collection of Ruysbroek's writings, translated from the original Flemish into Spanish. As he flipped through the book and pointed out particular passages that resonated with the writings of San Juan, I thought to myself, "I should not have been surprised."

Lázaro had discovered Ruysbroek in his youth, when he had been mentored by a popular Catholic priest in Matanzas. Padre Ramón had been a member of the same order as had been San Juan de la Cruz, the Carmelites. It was Ramón who introduced Lázaro (and many other Matanzas youth) to the wonders of mysticism, loaning or giving him books out of his vast collection, including the book of Ruysbroek's writings. While this particular Netherlands monk had not shown up in my seminary classroom, his influence had indeed been substantial, reaching into Germany and then into Spain and beyond, extending centuries later into this unassuming artist's home in the Matanzas neighborhood of Versalles.

Ruysbroek, Flanders
Wednesday, January 8, 1304 CE (Feast Day of St. Gúdula)
6:00 a.m.

Historians do not know Jan's surname; centuries after his death he would be known by the name of the village where he was born: Ruysbroek. The small village rested between two meandering rivers, the Scheldt and its tributary, the Dijle. Animal paths followed the sloping landscape between the rivers and through the woods; these paths later became walking trails for humans, and the trails eventually became roads for carts and carriages and cars. Eleven-year-old Jan loved to follow the trails with his mother. Ever since he was a toddler, he had made a habit of rising early to accompany her on her devotional walks. Every morning she would take him to special spots beside the Dijle to pray and read him Bible passages and tell him stories of the saints. A devout and pious woman, she found her young son's devotion admirable, and saddled him with that nickname—"Admirable"—a name that stuck even after his gaining sainthood. Saint Jan the Admirable.

The Admirable loved to hear the stories; his favorite was of Saint Gúdula. She had lived five centuries earlier in Flemish Brabant, and gained fame for her early morning prayers at the St. Salvator Church in Moorsel. As legend would have it, she would make her way to the church each morning before the cock's crow, and all along her journey, the devil would extinguish the flame of her lantern, but each time he put out the light, Gúdula's lamp would immediately rekindle. Jan's earliest memory was of his mother telling him this story at the riverside on a particularly cold winter morning, when the winds threatened to extinguish his own lamplight. He must have been three years old. Her vivid description of the devil-defying golden light rekindling time and time again struck a deep chord within him.

It was at that moment, in hearing that story, that he experienced the first twinges of an inner tension, the sharp conflict of the "should I stay or should I go?" question, although he did not yet have the understanding nor the vocabulary to conceptualize his troubling angst. He was nonetheless filled with an aching desire to go and find this saint and live close to her light. Nothing could be more important. But being a mama's boy, he was also filled with the desire to continue nestling in her bosom, smelling her familiar scent, hearing her voice as she filled his imagination with the stories of faith. The tension and the angst would stay with him for years to come.

Jan always asked to hear the Saint Gúdula story whenever he and his mother reached a particular place along the Dijle riverbank, a spot that was lined with fallen trees, the product of a major wind storm some years earlier. The trunks of the fallen trees had over the years become covered with "tremella delisquescens," a fungus whose bright yellow flower was known to the Flemish as "Sinte Goedele's Lampken" (St. Gúdula's Lantern), because not even the harsh winter winds could extinguish its shimmering light. It was the earliest of all the flowers to bring color to the Ruysbroek countryside, opening its first blooms in the dead of winter, sometime in January after Epiphany. Jan's own life-changing epiphany, the moment when he resolved his internal conflict of staying and going, happened on January 8th in the eleventh year of his life.

The 8th of January was a special day for Jan and his mother; it was the feast day of St. Gúdula. They made sure to have their morning prayers and lessons at the special spot on the riverbank, hoping and praying along the way that some of the golden blooms would have opened. Sure enough, on this particular January morning in the year 1304, the trunks were indeed dotted with dew-covered petals of St. Gúdula's Lantern. The sight of this moved Jan to his core; he could not explain what was happening inside his heart and mind. He had never seen anything so beautiful; it was as if the Saint herself was sitting there, laughing at the devil whose fierce January breaths could not extinguish the light of the flowers. When his mother finished the prayers and lessons, Jan asked if he could stay. She could tell by his eyes that his heart was so full, that he needed more time in contemplation and prayer, so she left him, trusting that God would protect him even as St. Gúdula had been protected so many times in her morning prayers.

Jan's mother could not have foreseen what happened next, and we don't know how admirable she felt his actions were that day. For as he sat there in silent prayer, contemplating the beauty of the flowing river and the radiant flowers on its bank, he suddenly heard a voice in the depths of his soul, a voice telling him it was time to leave. The voice directed him to go north, and to steer clear of the well-worn paths. Years later he would refer to this as his first "wayless" journey.

He walked through the woods, following the Dijle's course until it joined the Scheldt, and then he followed that river upstream until it met another tributary, the Zenne, and then followed the Zenne until it reached the walls of the Great Swamp village ("Great Swamp" is the etymological root meaning of the place name "Brussels"). There he found the St. Gúdula Church. At St. Gúdula's he found his uncle, Jan Hinckaert, who served as priest for this parish. Young Jan had followed the instructions of his inner voice, without giving any warning or explanation or bidding goodbye to his parents. He had simply started walking, until a few hours later, chilled to the bone, he knocked on the church door and was met by a rather startled uncle, Father Jan.

All the Admirable boy could tell the priest was that he wanted more than anything to be close to the Saint, whose bones were interred there behind the altar. He wanted to live close to her light, and he wanted to share her devotion. The priest obliged, mentoring and tutoring the saint-in-making until he was ordained to the priesthood thirteen years later. Among his parishioners was his mother, who, once discovering the whereabouts of her missing son, went to fetch him, and upon hearing the story of his conversations with her brother (Father Jan), gave thanks to God and moved there as well, to observe his growth into the vocation.

Jan the Admirable continued working alongside his uncle for twenty-six years, and perhaps he would have stayed there his entire life, close to Gúdula's bones, were it not for two other inner voices that began claiming his attention. One had to do with a growing controversy in the surrounding community. A group of radicals, calling themselves the Brethren of the Free Spirit, were causing trouble, chiefly through the writings of a woman among the Brethren, Bloemardinne, who was propagating heretical ideas of licentiousness through popular pamphlets written in the native tongue.

The elder Father Jan, who had discovered that his mentee had a gift for writing, enlisted his Admirable namesake to engage in the conflict and write his own pamphlets, challenging and correcting the Free Spirit errors.

This he did, carefully addressing every theological misconception, until he discovered, through the inner voice, that this was not his calling. This voice assured him that the fire of Gúdula's lantern would not be extinguished by any Free Spirit, no matter how heretical, and that the lantern did not need his well-crafted arguments to re-kindle the wick. If there was any battle to be fought, it would be between the Free Spirits and the Holy Spirit. Jan felt a growing desire to leave, to abandon the world of theological dispute and to disengage from such unnecessary striving.

The second inner voice, like the first, was telling him that something was not right in his world. The village of the Great Swamp had steadily grown in population, until now it was a fortified town of several thousand people. The new arrivals had been recruited to come and lend their muscle and sweat to a mammoth task: drying out the land. The soggy peat soil of Brussels, like that of Ruysbroek and like that of much of the Netherlands, was not useful for anything more than small, subsistence gardening and small herd shepherding. Yellow irises and roses of every color might thrive in this soil, but large-scale agriculture could not. The ancient voice of Cain, with its accompanying impulse to civilize, to conquer and control the land, was irresistible. The back-breaking work of digging canals to drain the swamp thus captured the imagination of the populace, who saw it as an opportunity to convert a soggy hell into a dry and glorious civilization.

A growing sense of caution and wariness began to consume Jan the Admirable as he watched this work steadily progress over the years. It would not be a play on words to say that he had a "sinking feeling," for this is literally what he felt. Without having any means to measure or validate his intuition, he was nonetheless certain that the earth was sinking beneath him. What the people were doing was wrong. It was madness, and his sensation proved to be right. As the project of drying out the peat became successful, over the next few decades the land slowly sank, until much of the Netherlands found itself below sea level. It was an ecological catastrophe that led to centuries of constant work, constructing and maintaining dykes and dams and canals, utilizing windmills and later steam engines to siphon out the water.

These two voices of discontent, one having to do with controversy in the religious world, the other with controversy in the physical world, combined to convey a clear message, as clear as the one he had heard as a child on the chilly banks of the Dijle: "Leave. Get away." He was consumed with the desire to find a place where neither scandalous spirits of so-called freedom nor scandalous spirits of so-called civilization would compete with his longing for a simple union with God.

Jan the Admirable left the parish in January of 1343, choosing again the feast day of Gúdula for his departure. He headed to the woods and made the conversion from Father Jan to Brother Jan, joining the hermitage of Groenendael in the neighboring forest of Soignes. It was a piece of earth yet to be touched by heretical spirits of license nor by arrogant spirits of civilization. To his delight, what he did find in the forest was a trove of *tremella delisquescens*, as the fungi had long ago found the fallen trees of the forest floor to be an accommodating space to thrive. Jan knew he was at home when he arrived at Groenendael and saw the bright yellow flowers of Saint Gúdula's Lantern blooming all around.

The priest-turned-monk spent the rest of his life engaging in admirable work there at the hermitage, labor both secular and sacred that would reverberate throughout the centuries and throughout the world. On the secular side, in order to sustain a modest livelihood, he and the brothers began brewing beer. Jan had always displayed a keen interest in the natural sciences, and through some experimentation there in the makeshift woodland brewery, he made the quite admirable discovery (at least it was admired by beer lovers near and far) that the wild yeast and bacteria of the *tremella delisquescens* fungi served to ferment a stout, sweet beer that to their palates was far superior to the popular German recipes, which relied on cultivated strains of brewer's yeast. In homage to his beloved Saint, Jan named their craft beer "lampken," (over the centuries the name would morph into "lambic," known worldwide in modern times as Belgium's signature beer). Its distinctive dry and cider-like taste quickly caught on, so that the only poverty the brothers of Groenendael suffered was due to their vows, not to any lack of gainful employment.

On the sacred side, Jan's other admirable work in the forest of Soignes involved his putting pen to paper, recording his thoughts on mysticism and the contemplative life. When the Admirable wasn't in the brewery, he could almost always be found wandering through the forest, tablet in hand, ready to write whenever the holy muse struck. Some of the Admirable's formally trained theologian friends confessed that they were at times uncomfortable with what the muse inspired in the wandering mystic, as there were touches of pantheism and universalism woven throughout the devotional thoughts and prayers: "All creatures are God in God. . . Everything in creation and everything in humanity exists eternally in God. . . God in the depths of us, receives God who comes to us: it is God contemplating God." Despite the misgivings of the learned theologians, the collection of Brother Jan's ample writings touched and influenced the lives of contemplatives to come, such as Thomas á Kempis and San Juan de la Cruz, as well as saints yet to be venerated, such as my friend and spiritual guide Lázaro Ceballos.

❖ ❖ ❖

Matanzas, Cuba
Wednesday, October 12, 2019 CE
8:00 a.m.

Lázaro and I regularly take walks together. One of our routes, which starts at the Kairos Center, begins with two hundred and sixteen steps down to Narvaez, a pedestrian boulevard which runs alongside the San Juan River. Then we walk west for five hundred and twenty-five steps, until we reach the point where the San Juan feeds into the Bay of Matanzas. Another forty-two steps takes us across the Vigía bridge, and then we have another twelve hundred and sixty-eight steps along the *malecón* (seaside walkway) that follows the northern shore of the bay until we reach the Playa neighborhood. There we find our turnaround point: the life-size statue of the Dutch pirate Piet Heyn gazing out on the bay. On one of these walks, Lázaro stopped at the San Juan to tell me about his earliest memory. He said he must have been around three years old when his father took him on an early morning walk, leaving Versalles at sunrise and making their way east to the city center, walking past the famed Sauto Theater until they reached Narvaez; it was at that moment when young Lázaro saw the San Juan River for the first time.

He described the experience to me: "I had never seen this river. That day, we were walking on the sidewalk alongside Narvaez street—this was back when it was still a street, not a pedestrian walkway. It was quite early in the morning, and the surface of the river was covered in a dense fog that reached to the bay. The sun burning through the fog revealed a white ball (I did not realize that it was a buoy), with a colorful flag above it, and when I saw that scene—the river, the lifting fog, the flag—I felt something that I could not explain. An immense joy. It was so, so intense, that I closed my eyes, because I could not bear so much beauty. My father saw that I had closed my eyes, and he laughed. After we left the sidewalk, I could not look back at the river, because it provoked this sensation that I had never before felt. Incredible. My father never knew. I didn't know how to explain it to him."

Lázaro explained to me that this was not the only time he was struck by ineffable beauty in his childhood. It seemed that everywhere he went, there was some new image that left him in awe, a deer at the nearby zoo, the framboyán tree in its bright red bloom, so that he kept having to close his eyes to keep from fainting from the dizziness such sights provoked. There were no words to explain it. In fact, this state of speechlessness was so constant, that for years his parents feared that Lázaro suffered from some kind of developmental disability. "My mother took me to a doctor, then to a psychologist, to see what the problem was. I was not communicative. I didn't relate to others; my life was very closed."

It was not until his ninth year, when he discovered a love for the martial arts and a group of friends to share that pastime with, that he became conversant. "One day everything changed, when my father took me to join a group of children who were practicing karate in the industrial zone, in a school called The Dynamo Captain San Luis. Suddenly, my life completely opened, through those exercises."

The other life-changing event for Lázaro was his discovery of el valle, the valley that would become a magical refuge for him for many years. The discovery happened when some of his friends told him they had discovered a chirimoya grove. "That is one of my favorite fruits. So I went with my friends, and sure enough, there it was, acres filled with row after row of chirimoya trees. This was at the edge of the valley. Some time later, after we had gone to enjoy the sweet treat several times, we ventured further, to see what was beyond the grove. There it was, the most beautiful valley imaginable. There's no way I can describe it; you have to be there to know its magic."

Over the past year, Lázaro and I have planned several excursions to hike to the mountain ridge above his neighborhood, and make our way to the valley so that I can indeed come to know its magic. Every single time we have planned the day-long outing, something has prevented us. Rain. Illness. Unexpected work project. Each time my longing to see what he has described has gotten stronger, and the image in my mind has grown, to the point that it has become something of a Shangri-La, an El Dorado, a Holy Grail, a mysterious place of legend, and I will have to continue planning the quest.

When Lázaro was around fourteen, he and some of his martial arts friends discovered another practice, aikido, and they began hiking to the valley on a daily basis to practice their newfound art. He would eventually become the instructor, rising to the level of black belt. As we walked along the bay there in the Playa neighborhood, he began describing this group of friends, the bonds they forged in the valley. As the years progressed, the valley took on added significance as it became a destination for hikes with Padre Ramón, from whom he and his friends would learn the practices of contemplative spirituality. For Lázaro, there was a seamless connection between what he had learned in practicing aikido and what he learned from San Juan de la Cruz and Jan Ruysbroek. The valley provided a space for oriental and occidental streams of spirituality to flow together.

I asked Lázaro what happened to this group of friends, if they still got together, and he lamented that he was the only one still in Cuba. They had all made the decision sometime along the way to leave. I asked if he had ever thought about leaving, and he said no, it was not something he could ever imagine doing. One of his aikido friends, Juanito, had lived in a really nice home in Pastorita, not too far from where we were walking. Juanito had suffered the loss of a brother many years earlier, and Lázaro had become something of a new brother for him. When Lázaro and Tamara's firstborn, Lazarito, was barely a year old, Juanito and his family had pressured them to leave Cuba.

Lázaro described the scene: "It was 1992, the day before there was to be a mass exodus from the island, thousands of people leaving in boats for Miami. I went to visit Juanito and his family. It was his mother who told me of their plans to leave, and she said to me, 'Lázaro, come with us; bring Tamarita and the baby.' I said, 'No, I'm staying. I don't want to leave, I don't want to leave my country. The valley—I know every rock, every tree, every step—I can't leave it.' She kept insisting, but no amount of pressure from her or from my friend could convince me otherwise. This was a very well-known family in Matanzas, and they lived a comfortable life here. But they all left. She, her husband, and their son, my good friend—my brother. The boat was very large. They left with another family, and they wanted so much to take us with them. But I could never leave my homeland. I never heard from him or from the family again."

We walked for several minutes in silence, allowing the memory of loss and the grief of the story to do its work. I looked out on the bay and imagined the scene of a large boat carrying families away. I wondered what became of them, and why they had decided never to communicate with their hometown friend. The mood lightened as we reached our destination, the statue of Piet Heyn, where Lázaro always paid homage to the Dutch pirate with a bow and a touch on the boot. He rose up and gave me a smile, and we began the walk back home.

Matanzas Bay
Friday, March 28, 1628 CE
9:30 a.m.

Piet Pieterszoon Heyn was born and raised in Rotterdam, where the Meuse River spills into the North Sea. Ships and shipbuilding were the life of the community, and Piet, being the son of a sea captain, never had a doubt as to his life's destiny. Dutch history books refer to this national hero as a privateer, which is a nice way of saying "pirate" (this was back in the day when governments would commission and authorize pirates to capture enemy merchant shipping). Piet became a sailor in his early teens, suffering through several years of extreme motion sickness. Just about the time his body adjusted to sea life, he was captured by the Spanish and suffered eight years of galley slavery, four of these years on a ship that regularly anchored in the harbors of Matanzas and Havana. After being liberated in a prisoner exchange, Piet climbed the ladder of piracy (privateering) until he gained the rank of Admiral, doing bidding for the Dutch West India Company, capturing Brazilian and Portuguese ships to gain an upper hand in two lucrative industries: sugar and the trans-Atlantic slave trade. After some time (historians don't know how long), he rejected the latter, and began speaking out against the institution of slavery.

Piet felt like everything that had happened to him in his life had prepared him for the fateful spring day of 1628, when he gained fame for defeating the Spanish in the Battle of the Bay of Matanzas. Four Spanish galleons were anchored there in the bay, so heavily laden with silver that the treasure blocked many of the ship's gun ports, making for a relatively nonviolent "battle." Piet Heyn's fleet began making their entrance into the bay mid-morning, effectively blocking passage and laying siege to the Spanish ships. Between the booty taken there and that looted from other Spanish ships in Havana, Piet Heyn returned to Holland with over eleven million guilders (the Dutch dollar) worth of silver. Elementary school children and drunken university students alike still sing a popular song in praise of the pirate's capture of the Spanish silver fleet in the Matanzas Bay.

There is a curious footnote to the story that doesn't show up in the song: Admiral Heyn neither executed nor took prisoner the enemy captain or crew of the defeated Spanish fleet. Instead, he asked them what they would like to do, where they would like to go. The captain said they needed to get to Havana, where they would rendezvous with others of the defeated fleet and seek a way back to Spain. Piet Heyn provided them with sufficient supplies for the sixty-mile march to Havana, and speaking in fluent Spanish (a skill he gained from his time as a slave), he gave them precise directions on how to get there. Perhaps that's enough reason to bow and touch the boot of this privateer of the Caribbean.

Matanzas, Cuba
Tuesday, December 15, 2020 CE
2:00 p.m.

Today was another one of those days that Lázaro and I had scheduled to hike to the ever more elusive valley. The weather forecast was promising, but our luck not so much. Kim and I had received the news a few days prior that our visas would not be renewed for another year, and we only had two weeks to prepare for a trip back to the states, where we would have to re-apply for a new visa. We learned yesterday that in order to board the plane for the states, we had to get the PCR test for COVID, asap. So the hike had to be tabled yet again, replaced with a trip to the International Health Clinic in Varadero, where foreigners have to go to be tested. We got back around mid-day, and as a consolation, I called up Lázaro to see if he wanted to meet up for coffee. Around 2:00 we met up at a coffee shop on Liberty Square.

Had we waited a few days, we could definitely have made a point to enjoy our espressos at a new coffee shop I would discover on Saturday, the day before our trip. I was on my way back to the Kairos Center from a fruit-less search for fruits and vegetables (no vendors to be seen on this day) to add to our "last supper" table with friends, when I saw that a new coffee shop had opened on Manzaneda Street, just a couple of blocks (less than two hundred steps) from the Center. I pride myself in knowing where every little "particular" (privately run) coffee shop is within a twenty-minute walk in every direction. I laughed when I saw the new sign tacked above this family's front door, "Amsterdam Café."

I walked into the living room-now-turned coffee shop and asked the woman serving up the nectar of the gods if she was from Holland. She politely said no, and nodded toward a woman at the back table, who turned out to be the proprietor. "So are you from Holland?" I asked. She smiled and said no, that her son was living there now, and that his wife and her grandchildren were from Amsterdam. She asked if I was Dutch, and I said no, but I had a good friend who traveled there some time ago and I would love to bring him by for a cup of coffee. She got out her cell phone and began showing me photos of her son and his family there in Holland, and how she would love to visit there someday and see those beautiful canals. Add that to my to-do list for my return to Cuba—café with Lázaro at the Amsterdam Café.

As it was, we settled for coffee in the park, and as always, I waited to see where the muse would take Lázaro in his story-telling. Among the treasures of the afternoon was his description of the time he did travel to Holland, with the musical group Agua Viva, back in 2009. Paco Rodés, pastor emeritus of the church and founder/President of the Kairos Center, had worked with one of the seminary professors, Hans Spinder, to arrange a trip to do some concerts in Hans' hometown of Utrecht. Before the trip, Hans and his spouse, Wil, had asked each person in the group to think of one thing they would like to do while in Holland, and he would make sure that it got in the itinerary. Lázaro had an immediate response: "I want to see the Van Gogh museum."

And so it happened that Lázaro got to see original works of his artistic luminary. While the other members of the group went to visit the Anne

Frank house, he and Paco took a car for the forty-minute ride north. He describes the experience: "This was one of the great longings of my life. Because Van Gogh was the main source of inspiration in my art. How was it possible that I would get to see his works up close? And suddenly, I was there. The Sunflowers, the Night Café; they were all there, right in front of me. The colors, everything, so incredible."

The museum would have much information on these and other famous works, analyses and reflections on Van Gogh's obsession with vivid color, especially the strong sulphur yellow hues of the sun. Lázaro recalls the challenge of being there, with so much to see and a limited time in which to see it. "You can imagine that when I entered the museum, I did not want to miss any detail. I had audio-phones to guide, but had to remove them, because they were too fast. It did not make sense, rushing from one room to another, from one work to another. Because I wanted to stay in front of each one, longer than the recorded guide."

Lázaro continued describing his visit, and his fascination with a particular painting: "It is a wonderful work; there is a table and a family of five humble peasants eating potatoes. So much sobriety, so much simplicity in that room with the table. The attention goes immediately to the heat of the potatoes. And to the hunger of the people. I was filled with so much emotion. Even though my inclination as an artist goes toward the intense colors—which is what Van Gogh is famous for—nevertheless it was that painting, with its narrow range of dark earth tones, that impacted me the most. The faces of those poor peasants, the flesh tones similar to that of the dusty potatoes—it is nothing like his other paintings. To achieve the contrasts through light and dark, to create that atmosphere, it is truly a magical work."

I wondered later if Lázaro was drawn to this dark canvas because of his own attraction toward the spirituality of darkness; Saint John of the Cross' *Dark Night of the Soul* is his primary source for the deepest truths of contemplation and mysticism. I am sure he and Saint John would both resonate with Van Gogh's own travels through the soul's dark night. Young Vincent had early on felt a calling to ministry, following in the footsteps of his father, who was a pastor. But he found he was not cut out for the rigorous theological studies of Latin and Greek and Calvin. After failing miserably at the academic life, he made his way to the poor mining district of Borinage to work as a lay preacher. He so wanted to identify with the humble people, to be in solidarity with them in their struggles, that he chose to sleep on planks in a makeshift hut, just as the miners did, and he did not bathe, as they did not. He tended to the sick and did his best to share the gospel, but soon the simple folk grew suspicious of this wild-looking preacher and sent him on his way.

Dejected, Van Gogh made pilgrimage from town to town seeking purpose for his life, first Etten, then The Hague, and it was then that his focus shifted. He took to sketching the countryside and the peasants who lived there. The shadow side of his life intensified as his relationship with the Holy Spirit began to be enhanced by his relationship with spirits of another kind: he started his lifelong habit of imbibing absinthe. Many biographers suspect that this contributed to the madness for which he became known. His hallucination-filled journeys eventually took him and his sketch pad to the land of San Gúdula in the province of Brabant, and it was there in the village of Nuenen that the young artist began shaping the dark canvas that he would later consider his finest work, *The Potato Eaters*.

I suspect that another of the attractions of this painting for Lázaro is the setting: a family eating around a table. Kim and I found that our Wednesday evening ritual meal at their home was so essential for our spirits for the simple reason that they as a family still eat together (and converse, and sing, and raise toasts) around the table. It may sound trite, but sharing table together is a lost art, and Lázaro's family is recovering that art. It is no surprise that one of his passions as an artist is painting scenes of the Last Supper; he gifted us with one of these works on the last of our Wednesday gatherings before our trip to the states, telling us it represented a promise that we would soon be back around the table together.

Our afternoon café conversation on the Holland trip turned toward what Lázaro considers to be another major shift in his journey of life. It was in Utrecht that he met Arjan, the host pastor of one of the churches where they visited, and a prison chaplain. Arjan took the group on a tour of one of the prisons where he worked, and it was on that tour when something quite unexpected began stirring in Lázaro. He began feeling the first inkling of a calling that he would soon be answering, into chaplaincy work. Soon after their return to Cuba, Paco would recognize this calling, and invite Lázaro to join him in starting the island's first prison chaplaincy program.

There in Utrecht, Lázaro engaged in many conversations with Arjan about the nature of his work, and the two of them forged a lasting friendship. Lázaro laughed as he told me about the parting gift he had received from his new friend. It was a beaded prayer bracelet, complete with a written guide on how to use it in times of prayer. When he came home from the Holland trip, Lázaro paid a visit to his grandmother to tell her about the adventure, and something told him he should give her this bracelet. He smiled as he continued the story.

"Not too long after, grandma found there was more to the gift than meets the eye. She was fond of gambling, whether with bingo or dominos or other table games, but she particularly prone to play the numbers in the daily bolita lottery. She confided to me that whenever she prayed with those beads, a number would pop into her head. On a hunch, she started putting money on the number that her prayer bracelet revealed, and behold, it worked every time! Grandma was able to buy a television set, a fan, and also give money to me for the children, all from her prayer beads. She finally put a stop to that particular mode of gambling when word got out to some of her friends, and she would be surrounded every day with neighbors who wanted to pray with her!"

Fairview, N.C.
Friday, December 25, 2020 CE
8:00 p.m.

I have thought a lot about Lázaro and his family today, during our Christmas in quarantine here in the western North Carolina mountains. For the past several years, Lázaro and Tamara and Yeni María have traveled with us to La Vallita for the holidays, to spend Christmas with Sila Reyna and her family. Last year Lázaro coordinated a major art project, designing a mural on the front of the house for everyone to help paint. I thought about how Sila would love the story of grandma's prayer beads and the lottery, given her own gamble with the bolita that led to her conversion to the faith.

We missed out on that, along with many other traditions, this year. As Kim and I lamented that we really had not thought about Christmas gifts for each other this year, I remembered one of the last things Lázaro shared with me of when we were finishing up our coffee conversation there at the park. It was a quote from an obscure (to me) Bulgarian spiritual guru, Omraam Mikhaël Aïvanhov, something I had heard Lázaro reference once before from a book on meditation and silence. The Omraam said that whenever people go abroad and visit foreign lands, they often bring back gifts to share with their loved ones. That's part of the beauty and joy of travel, bringing back these sometimes exotic keepsake gifts. Then the guru made his point: "We must go abroad every day, to find gifts and offer them to friends and loved ones. This 'abroad' refers to the inner silence; this is the other country, the foreign land. And when we return from this distant silence, we bring back many gifts, gifts of love, of understanding, of joy." Lázaro closed our time with this bon voyage: "That is the foreign trip that I make every day. You make it, too. We look forward to seeing what gifts you bring back to us."

Chapter 5

Walking with Luis and His French Ancestors

La libertad tiene alma clara
y solo canta cuando va batiendo alas.[1]

—SILVIO RODRÍGUEZ, YO TE QUIERO LIBRE

Matanzas
Sunday, October 27, 2019 CE
2:30 p.m.

"She wrote that it 1947!" Luis excitedly blared out to me as I sat across from him at his kitchen table, strewn with books, including a collection of Simeon de Beauvoir's writings. *Nowhere but in Cuba*, I thought, as I sat there in this darkened, humble dwelling with no running water that day (Matanzas' city water system being notorious for breakdowns), the aroma of a garlic braid hanging on the wall, a Hayden sonata emanating from the old transistor radio always tuned to Cuba's national classical music station, and this dear old man, eager as always to share his love of literature. His excitement on this day came from the work he was doing in translating one of the French existentialist's letters, in which she said:

1. Translated: "Freedom has a clear soul and only sings when it is beating its wings." Rodríguez, Silvio. "Yo te quiero libre." *Tríptico (Vol. 3)*. Polydor, 1984. Album.

> I want everything from life, I want to be a woman and to be
> a man, to have many friends and to have loneliness, to work
> much and write good books, and to travel and enjoy myself, to
> be selfish and to be unselfish. . .You see, it is difficult to get all
> which I want.

"Me too!" Luis said, and then went on to tell me about the time that
Simone de Beauvoir and her soul-mate Jean Paul Sartre came to visit Cuba,
early in the Revolution. Luis resonated with one of Sartre's quotes that he
was almost sure came from that visit, where the philosopher said that he was
a "traveller without a ticket." "That's me," he smiled, "on a journey, with no
destination in mind. It's a great adventure."

Fairview, N.C.
Tuesday, March 16, 2021 CE
12:52 p.m.

I finish a quick lunch of tomato soup and a banana sandwich, and
then walk down the twelve steps to my downstairs desk, where I have been
working on the book every day. I am working on this very chapter, review-
ing interview notes and doing background reading for the story of Luis
Pérez Martinto, a man who more than anyone I know embodies the French
aspects of Cuban culture. I open up my phone to check messages before
getting down to writing, and am devastated to read a short note from our
dear friend Yivi: "Luis Pérez died this morning."

As one of my closest friends, and one of the primary collaborators in
this project, Luis and I had kept in touch on a regular basis since December, through email. His messages were always a mixture of suggestions for
stylistic edits, and an overview of his latest reading material—he was eager
to translate Amanda Gorman's inaugural poem and wanted to find more
of her work. We had been out of touch in late February, as he had been
hospitalized for vertigo and a slight stroke. He wrote me when he got home,
saying, "I have greatly missed having your words of encouragement. . . . I
am emerging these days from the valley of shadows. Most of the time I have
to be seated or lying down. For me, this is torture. . . . I see that with Biden
everything will be the same as always. Too bad!"

That March 13 missive would be the last I heard from Luis. I will miss
him greatly.

Matanzas, Cuba
Friday, December 18, 2020 CE
3:00 p.m.

I don't usually think when I am leaving a friend's house that it might be the last time I will ever see him alive. I certainly had no thought of that when I made my weekly three hundred and eighty-nine step walk from our Calle Medio apartment to the home of Luis Pérez Martinto on Manzaneda Street. In my role as associate pastor of the church, I, along with Pastor Orestes and a team of leaders, had divided up the church membership by neighborhood, and we each took a section of the city with a set of members living there to deliver the weekly bulletin, with a liturgy to use for home worship during the quarantine. I had the neighborhoods on the western side of the city, and made my rounds on Fridays or Saturdays. Luis was the closest on my route, and I would either start or finish the journey with a stop at his home. During the first weeks of the pandemic, when the quarantine measures were more strict, these visits would take place with the two of us standing at his doorway, conversing six feet apart, as home visits were prohibited. It wasn't long, though, before the restrictions loosened, and we were able to sit and visit at his kitchen table.

These visits were always a highlight of my week, as Luis was a brilliant conversationalist, with philology and literature and cultural arts among his fields of expertise. When I shared with him my idea for this book, he was enthusiastic in his encouragement and volunteered to help me with my translation into Spanish. He was even more enthusiastic when I explained the format of featuring a representative from the various "mother countries" that make up Cuban culture. I asked if he would consent to be my French connection. A bona fide franco-file and professor of the French language, he was more than happy to comply. In many interviews Luis had shared stories of his travels, both within Cuba and abroad. It was on that that December day that he told me the story of his birth.

"My full name is Adrian Luis Pérez Martinto—I had a mother, you know." (I had heard Luis make this remark many times, whenever people referred to him as Luis Pérez; he was proud of his maternal last name). "My mother had decided that her firstborn, if a boy, would be called Adrian; this was the name of her great-great-grandfather who was the first to leave Spain for the new world." I learned that this Adrian, who was only a young teenager when he left, had long tired of the arguments in his family home. It was in the early 1800s, during the time of the French occupation, and Adrian's father, whose grandparents had come to Spain from France, was a committed *afrancesado*, a sympathizer with Bonaparte and the enlightened ideals of the French revolution. Adrian's maternal grandfather, who lived with them, was on the other side, a strict loyalist to the Catholic Church and the juntas of resistance. The war of words that filled the house every day matched the war of arms that raged throughout the country.

Adrian had no loyalty to either side of this civil war; something in his phase of teenage rebellion caused him to believe that both of the competing systems were despotic and power hungry. Neither his father nor his grandfather gave him leave to speak his mind, though. They did not want to hear of his longings to get out from under the thumb of any despot, be it an enlightened secular one or a Dark Ages papal version or an in-house dictatorship.

So it happened that the fourteen-year-old boy simply left home one day, without a word of explanation, and made his way to the docks, with as much food as he could muster stuffed inside his clothes. There he sneaked aboard one of the ships, hid in its hull, and decided to let fate determine his destination. Two months later, Adrian emerged from the ship and set foot in his new country, Cuba, where he would forge a new life and create a future for generations to come.

Luis brewed some espresso and as we enjoyed the afternoon merienda, he continued the story. "The name 'Luis' was not planned; it came about by accident, literally. You see, of all the steps I have taken in my life, the most important by far was one I didn't even make; it was one my mother made while I was only four months in the womb. And it wasn't really a step at all; it was a misstep. She was going out to get something from the bodega. It had been raining earlier in the day, and as soon as her foot hit the sidewalk, she slipped and fell hard. The fall knocked her unconscious. Some neighbors tended to her and got her to the maternity hospital, where the doctors examined her and told her the pregnancy was in jeopardy. They alerted her that her own life might be endangered if she continued the pregnancy, and advised her to consider an *interrupción* (the Cuban euphemism for miscarriage or abortion).

"My mother went home from the hospital, and against the doctor's advice, chose not to interrupt the pregnancy. She was a fervent pentecostal, having been a founding member of the Bethel church, and when her faith community learned of her situation, they anointed her with what they called a 'concert of prayer.'"

Luis' eye's twinkled and a mischievous smile came across his lips as he continued the story: "My mother, like many Cubans, liked to hedge her bets, when it came to matters of faith. Even though the pastor at Bethel had preached long and hard about how the African religions were demonic, my mother was not so sure. So, in addition to praying her pentecostal prayers, she went one day to see one of her neighbors, an Afro-Cuban woman known to be gifted in the art of healing. Mamá sensed that the 'concert of prayer' might be strengthened by the inclusion of some other voices."

Luis paused for a few moments, and appeared to be in deep contemplation. He then shared what was on his mind: "What I'm telling you now was a secret my mother kept for many years; I doubt she told anyone other than me. And I haven't told it to many people. The readers of your book will be among the first to know."

The santera welcomed Luis' mother into her home, and after hearing her story and concern about the dangers of continuing the pregnancy, the large black woman escorted her into a back room filled with the trappings of the Regla de Osha religion. The santera arranged the altar, and set out to do some anointing of her own. She prepared a ritual offering for Oshún, the orisha related to fertility, sweet water, and love. She then draped Luis' mother in yellow and gold cloths, Oshún's colors, and began chanting her prayers. She added some sea shells to the makeshift altar, and waited for an oracle to emerge.

Luis' mother would tell him that the few moments they waited in silence seemed like an eternity. Finally, the santera spoke, and the message from Oshún and the oracle was clear: a baby boy was destined to be born. "He will come with the waters," she said. The priestess then gave counsel that would mark Luis' life forever: "Note the day of his birth, for this child carries history in his bones. His saint will be his guide."

Luis continued, "My mother was aware that the Catholics kept a calendar of saints, with every day being a feast day for one saint or another. So, as she entered into the eighth month, and knew that the birth would not be long in coming, she again hedged her bet. She walked over to Versalles and paid a visit to Saint Peter's church, probably the only time she set foot in a Catholic Church, as the Bethel preacher warned that the Catholics were as demonic as the Afro-Cubans. Never mind, they had something she needed. She asked the priest about the calendar of saints, and inquired if she might get a copy of the August page. He obliged, and she took it home to consider what saint might mark the life of her son."

So it was that the baby boy who was to be Adrian Pérez Martinto became Adrian *Luis* Pérez Martinto. He indeed came with the waters, as his mother went into labor on a day of torrential rainfall, and gave birth at dusk while sheets of rain continued to fall. It was August 25, 1941. Luis' mother circled the day on the calendar the priest had given her. It was the feast day

of San Louis, aka King Louis IX, the only monarch of France to be canon-
ized by the Roman Catholic Church.

"I was a teenager, probably not much older than my ancestor Adrian,
when my mother told me the secret of my second name. It happened when
I became obsessed with a French singer, Edith Piaf, my first entree into the
world of French culture, which would become my life's passion. This world-
renowned singer had come to do a concert in La Habana, and it was tele-
vised. I was enthralled by this petite woman, who was not pretty, but who
had a voice that was completely mesmerizing. I thought she was singing to
me."

At this point Luis' eyes brightened as he began singing—in French—a
verse from "Sous le ciel de Paris" ("Under the Sky of Paris"), giving emphasis
to the line extolling love for the Île Saint Louis.

Luis' infatuation with Piaf, with her songs, with all references to
French life, including the Isle of Saint Louis and its namesake, was a sign to
his mother (as a good pentecostal, she was always on the lookout for signs).
So she confessed her secret, the meaning behind his name, a story that he
shared with me almost seventy years later.

Languedoc, France
Tuesday, August 25, 1248 CE
6:30 a.m.

For the first twenty years of his life, Adrien led the simple and satisfy-
ing life of a shepherd and cheesemaker in the Languedoc region of southern France. During his teen years he gained fame for producing the finest
roquefort ever to come out of that region's caves.[2] While Adrien had been
raised to be a faithful Catholic, he found his deepest devotion in tending
the sheep and turning their milk into the blue-veined hard cheese. A bright
sparkle came to his eyes whenever he saw his flock happily grazing on the
sunlit pasture grass. The same glimmer emerged whenever he sampled some
of the crumbly roquefort. While these pastoral pleasures were his primary
sources of inspiration, he did come to appreciate King Louis' more conven-
tional spirituality and religious zeal, especially when the King turned his
attention to the Cathar heretics of Languedoc. They were a strange bunch,
preaching the good and the bad news of not one but two gods, a benevolent
one and an evil one.

2. Roquefort and other blue cheeses were processed in dark, damp caves.

According to the Cathars, the bad god (the Old Testament deity) created the world and all that is in it. Which meant that the world and all that is in it was evil. The good god (the New Testament version) they identified as pure spirit, having nothing to do with the material world. For Adrien, none of this nonsense would have bothered him, "everyone to his own heresy," he used to say, except for two other peculiarities in the Cathar belief system: they prohibited the eating of cheese, and they prohibited sex, since both had to do with material pleasures, meaning they flowed from the evil god. "You can believe what you want," Adrien mused, "but don't mess with people's enjoyment of a good wheel of cheese. And if you're going to outlaw sex, well, then maybe the King doesn't need to send in the Inquisitors or the Crusaders after all; that kind of heresy will surely die on the vine."

In the medieval system, being a shepherd, which is to say, a peasant, meant that Adrien was beholden to the nobleman who owned the land, in his case it was lord Raoul de Soissons. Adrien found that Raoul was not so bad at lording it over people; the lord's real passion was in songwriting. He was a wannabe troubadour who wrote dozens of *chansons* (chant-like folk songs). Adrien would often catch himself singing some of the lord's verses while milking the sheep."When I see the leaf and flower" was a favorite, along with "When I see the red clay forming."

Adrien learned that he would be leaving the leaf and flower and clay of the pastoral life, as Raoul informed the peasants under his charge that they would soon be on the move. The King was summoning an army to join him in the seventh Crusade to recapture the holy city of Jerusalem, which had fallen to the Khwarazmians some four years earlier. So it was that early on a Tuesday morning in late August of 1248, a misty-eyed Adrien said goodbye to his sheep and set off to war. "I'll see you in Jerusalem!"

The shepherd left Languedoc with visions of the glories of war, hearing as he did the growing war cries accompanied by kettle drums and trumpets. In his mind's eye was the imagined face of their sworn enemy, Al-Salih, Sultan of Egypt, ruler of the infidels who had captured and desecrated the holy city of God. Ten thousand men, including Adrien, boarded ships and set off, making their first stop at Cyprus. The layover there lasted long enough for him to meet some of the locals, fall in love with the first Greek maiden who gave him the time of day, and engage in some of those very pleasures the Cathars would have forbidden. It was a short-lived love, though, as the Crusaders set sail again and landed in Egypt in June 1249, now with eighteen thousand soldiers, as Louis recruited all along the journey.

In their first major battle, King Louis' Crusaders captured Damietta, and there they heard the news that Sultan Al-Salih was dying of tuberculosis. They bided their time, waiting for the annual Nile flooding to abate, and set off for Cairo in November 20. There was a slow march along banks of Nile, accompanying the boats laden with supplies. It was on this march that Adrien began to learn the less than glorious nature of war.

While lord Raoul and the other noblemen could ride comfortably aboard their steeds, and invent chansons of battle victory, this was not the experience of Adrien and his fellow peasant recruits. For them, it was mostly slogging through the mud while dealing with dysentery (a condition that creates suffering enough for any individual who gets it, but imagine 5,000 men sharing the fate at the same time). Worse of all, though, were the memories of the way so many of his fellow soldiers had been brutally killed by his side in that first battle. The images of their wounded bodies were etched in Adrien's mind, and their death cries kept ringing in his ears.

Mansourah, Egypt
Thursday, Feb 8, 1250 CE
7:30 a.m.

Having learned of the Sultan's death, King Louis made a strategic decision to quickly cross the river and attack the leaderless enemy from behind. One of the Knights, his brother Robert of Artois, made the unfortunate bad decision to attack before all of the army had crossed the river. Adrien found himself and his fellow soldiers hemmed in, and he witnessed many of his fellow crusaders being massacred as the Muslims counterattacked. As he engaged in hand to hand combat, he felt a lance pierce through his shoulder, knocking him to the ground. As he rolled over and looked up, the last thing he would see in his life was the hoof of a stampeding horse coming down on his face. When he came to, he found himself in an Egyptian prison, blinded, under guard of the Marmeluk Baibars (who had formerly been enslaved bodyguards of the Sultan).

Adrien would spend two months in that Mansourah prison, until King Louis, who had been imprisoned himself, made ransom payments of 800,000 *bezants*, and negotiated release of the prisoners of war. Blind, with his right arm made useless from the lance injury, and at the point of starvation, he and his fellow failed Crusaders began the long journey back to France. He would not be going back to Languedoc, though. The injured were directed to Paris, where they would receive treatment in one of the hospitals the King had established. Adrien had never heard of a hospital, but was grateful to learn what it was when he arrived at the newly opened Quinze-Vingt, a three hundred bed hospital for blind persons. There he would receive the hospitality and compassion care of the Beguine sisters who served the facility at the bequest of King Louis.

The sisters gently treated his wounded eyes with oxymel, a salve made of vinegar and honey. While there was no hope in restoring his sight (short of a miracle), the salve did ease the piercing pain. Over the course of a year there in the hospital, the sisters helped Adrien learn to walk and navigate daily routines without sight, eventually taking him on excursions throughout the city, where he would experience the sounds of life along the Reine, along with the smells of incense in the Cathedral of Notre Dame, and his favorite destination of all, the recently constructed Saint-Chapelle, where he loved to go and kneel before the most holy of relics, Christ's crown of thorns, a gift Louis had received from the Emperor of Constantine in exchange for the payment of a debt.

Adrien left the hospital a year later, rehabilitated by the Beguines and ready to join the ranks of the Parisian beggars. He found his place on the streets of the Ile de la Cité, not far from Notre Dame. It didn't take him long to start wandering, though, as the urge toward adventure was not abated by blindness. Sounds and smells fascinated him, and sometimes attracted him to move in their direction. The most powerful aroma was that of the cow manure, emanating from the nearby Île aux Vaches (i.e., Cows' Island, the neighboring island that would, centuries later, be developed and re-named the Isle of Saint Louis). While the bovine aromas were distinct from the smell memory of his beloved sheep, they nonetheless filled him with nostalgia. Soon, he would make a daily pilgrimage, taking the 91 steps across the foot bridge (that would also one day be re-named for the King, the Pont San Louis), and spend the better part of every afternoon wandering through the fields and pastures of the Île aux Vaches. He loved talking to the herdsmen, arguing with them about the advantages of the ewe's roquefort versus the cow's camembert.

Several years later, he would have this same argument over which *from-age* reigns supreme with none other than King Louis himself, at the King's table. Louis, after spending four years in the Middle East following the failed Crusade, returned to Paris and dedicated himself to some of the practices that eventually earned him his sanctified status. He devoted himself to the life of the poor and was committed to doing all he could to alleviate their suffering. He regularly visited the hospitals, where he emptied bedpans and applied salve to wounds, along with offering prayers and words of encouragement. He took daily walks around the Île de la Cité and the Île aux Vaches, encountering the poorest of the poor and inviting them to dine with him.

When the beggars arrived at the palace at the appointed mealtime, the King would meet them in the foyer and wash their feet before entering the expansive dining room. The first time Adrien experienced this *lavatorio de pies*, something stirred in his heart. It was as if the horrors of war were being bathed in forgiveness, and a tender love for this crusading King replaced resentment. Had someone looked at Adrien's face as the King's hands were gently handling his dirty and calloused feet, they might have seen a miraculous glimmer briefly return to those long-dead eyes.

At the table, the King proved to possess greater skill at engaging in conversation than he had in waging war. He would question first one beggar and then another about things that might interest them, nudging them gently out of their timid silence, and patiently listen as stories began to emerge. When he addressed Adrien, who was seated to the King's left, he placed his hand on the blind man's shoulder, and simply said, "Friend, I want to know how to pray for you. If you had three desires in this world, what would they be? Tell me, and I will pray for God to grant your wishes." Adrien sat in silence for a few moments, pondering the question. The other beggars around the table sat in silence, curious to hear what the desires would be.

Adrien finally spoke, "First of all, I would like awaken some morning and see what the sun looks like when it rises over the Seine. Second, I wish to find love, to marry and have children. And third—"(with this Adrien paused, and a hint of a smile passed across his lips), "I would like for the King to be able to savor the taste of some good cheese; if there were but a wheel of Languedoc's roquefort here, this table would be complete." Mouths dropped open around the table at this last desire, in fear that this would be taken as an insult, but the King quickly broke the brief silence with a resounding roar of laughter, and a blessing of "well done!" accompanied by a few strong pats on Adrien's back. "Those are three decent desires, to be sure, and I would wager that at least two of my three prayers will be answered."

So it happened that on one of Adrien's subsequent visits to the King's table, he discovered that Louis had spent part of his day visiting the House of the Felles-Dieu, a refuge for reformed prostitutes. Once again Adrien was seated next to the King, but this time, seated to the blind man's left was not a fellow beggar, but a woman named Blanche. The King made conversation about her name, which was the same as his mother's. Adrien found himself to be mute, unable to think of a single word to add to the conversation. As he sat and listened, he tried to imagine, from the way this woman talked, what her facial features might look like.

The King's servants soon began bringing food to the table, first bread, and wine, and then a sudden aroma reached Adrien's keen nostrils and brought his silent tongue back to life. "No! It can't be!" The King exploded in another burst of laughter, as he took knife in hand and cut the first wedge from the wheel of the blue roquefort, putting it on a slice of bread and handing it to Adrien. He did the same for Blanche, and then for himself, before raising his chalice of wine and offering a toast, "Here's to the God who answers prayers!" Once again, a sparkle shone in Adrien's blank eyes, and he suddenly found himself more curious about what Blanche thought of the taste, than the King's own critique.

Their marriage was soon to come, and in their daily routine, Blanche came to love the midnight hour most of all. After love-making, she would wait for Adrien to fall into a deep sleep. She lay there in the darkness, eyes wide open for fear she might, too, fall asleep, waiting the two hours it generally took for the dreams to enter Adrien's mind. They never failed to come, and they were always the same, visions of sheep grazing in sunlit grass. The nocturnal visions always caused him to sing in his sleep, chansons of leaf and flower and red clay forming. Their night-time ritual produced three children. The firstborn they named for the other love of Adrien's life, Louis. The second was a daughter, Melania. The third was another son, who took his father's name.

This last, like many youngest children of the family, grew up with a wandering spirit, eager to see the world. It happened in his late teenage years that the brothers of a nearby monastery called for a pilgrimage to the Camino of Santiago, and this gave him leave to follow his heart's desire. He walked the Camino, reached the shrine of the apostle in Galicia, and never made the return pilgrimage. So it was that one branch of the family tree came to grow in Spain. Over the generations, there would be more Adriens, as the blind shepherd's story was told and re-told and sons were named in his honor. A few centuries later, there would still be Adriens in the family line, even though the stories had been long forgotten. One of them would discover the same urge for adventure, and at fourteen years of age, would leave the family home without a word to hide himself in the hull of a ship, bound for who knows where.

Matanzas, Cuba
Monday, April 15, 2019 CE
6:00 p.m.

It was Monday of Holy Week and I was already tired from the liturgical events that had started the day before. The next two days would involve a spring workshop for children, then a foot-washing service on Holy Thursday, the seven last words of Christ service on Friday, a guided pilgrimage for youth on Saturday, and up early on Sunday for the sunrise service. I was taking a pre-dinner siesta in the apartment when I got a phone call from Luis.

He was terribly upset, and asked if I could come by and see him. I asked what was wrong, but he couldn't talk without weeping, so I said I'd be right over. I made the familiar 389-step walk, and he invited me in and told me the news that the Notre Dame Cathedral had caught fire; he had seen images of the spire collapsing on the evening news. He began describing what it had been like for him to visit this iconic site, something he had dreamed of his whole adult life. A Parisian friend of his, who had visited Cuba on many occasions, had gifted him with a two-month trip just three years prior, from May to July of 2016.

As he talked, an idea occurred to me. "Luis, I missed your birthday last year; I was in the States. Remember that year when we were in Varadero on your birthday and Kim and I treated you to a piña colada, and we said that was something we needed to repeat? Well, let's do it now. I think we need to go and raise a toast to the people of Paris and their tremendous cathedral, and say a prayer that the damage will be minimal and its restoration swift. I know just the place." He was game, and got himself together to follow me to my destination. We walked forty-five steps down Manzaneda, turned up Contreras, and took another one hundred and sixty-seven steps to reach Liberty Park. There at the corner, I pointed out where it was we needed to be that evening. It was a bar on Milanes, across the park, in the newly restored Louvre Hotel (actually, the hotel part, originally built in 1904, was still under re-construction, but the bar was fully functional). The Louvre is one of the iconic representations of French influence on Matanzas architecture and culture.

We sat and ordered the over-priced piña coladas, and I told Luis that I had never had the chance to hear him describe his trip to Paris, and would love to hear about it. "You've told me about Notre Dame, but what were some of your other favorite experiences there?" This is all it took for Luis to begin reminiscing with great joy. He had gone with a list of must see destinations. "I won't bore you with the obvious ones," he said. "You know all about the art of the Louvre, the grandeur of the Eiffel Tower, and while all that was every bit as good as I could have imagined, I was more interested in some places off the beaten path." And so the journey started, with Luis masterfully going from subject to subject, one thing leading to another, and I wound up with a history lesson that more than made up for the price of the cocktails.

It came as no surprise that Luis was interested to visit a jazz spot where Nina Simone had sung—"She was the high priestess of soul, you know," and I was happy to be able to tell him something about her that he didn't know—"She was born in North Carolina, just down the mountain from where we live, in Tryon." He was surprised to learn that, and continued, talking about how she had a following here in Matanzas; they even used her music as background for an original play in the Teatro de Estaciones. He went on to talk about visiting the Café de Flor, one of the regular hangouts of James Baldwin.

"I loved imagining the young black writer sitting there in that same café, having escaped the racism he suffered in New York. I even found a copy of *Giovanni's Room* in a nearby bookstore, and sat there in the Café, drinking coffee and nibbling on fromage blanc with hot French bread while I re-read the book, there in the very place where it had been born in Baldwin's mind. You know the book, of course." I sheepishly confessed that I didn't; while I had read a lot of James Baldwin's works, this one I had missed. "Oh, it's one of his best; it's about a gay man in Paris. Imagine that!"

From there Luis went on to tell me about José White, one of the most famous of Matanzas' nineteenth-century classical musicians and composers. The Afro-Cuban violinist had left his home country, as had Nina Simone and James Baldwin, for the lure of Paris, and had made quite a mark in European music of the era. "The saddest day of the trip, for me," Luis shared, "was my visit to the cemetery of Boulogne-sur-Seine, where he was buried in March of 1918. The family vault was in great disrepair, and its surroundings overgrown with weeds. The first thing I did when I got back to my hotel was to write letters to the Ministry of Culture in Cuba, and to the Mayor of Paris, lamenting what I had found, pleading with them to give attention to José White's burial place, to maintain it with the honor and respect he deserves. It was only two years away from the centennial of his death, and I can only hope my letters provoked some action."

From where we were sitting there in the Louvre bar, we could look across the park and see the entrance to the music hall Salón José White, another recently restored space in Matanzas' central square. "If only Roque[3] could have been in Paris and done the same at Boulogne-sur-Seine," my friend fantasized.

"But do you know what was my favorite thing to do in Paris?" I nodded "no" to his rhetorical question, and he filled me in. "I took a stroll every morning to the Île de Saint Louis. I can't explain the feeling exactly, but the first time I left Notre Dame and crossed the Pont Saint Louis to get from the Île de la Cité to the island bearing my name, I had the strangest sensation that I was at home. I could have just as easily been walking down Manzaneda or Calle Medio."

I had not yet heard the story of his mother's secret, the challenging pregnancy and the counsel of the Santera about this baby boy who would be bringing the history of a saint with him into this world. Had I known, the strange sensation Luis described would have made perfect sense. As it

---

3. Sergio Roque, the Matanzas artist who designed and oversaw the restoration of the Salon José White.

was, he filled me in on some reading he did while in the Chapel of Saint Louis, learning about the blessed King, how he reformed the judicial system so that all would have a better chance at being treated justly. He was the first to introduce the presumption of innocence in criminal procedure, and he eliminated the trial by ordeal (made famous in our lifetime by Monty Python), replacing it with trial by jury. While the King was not a pacifist (after all, he led two Crusades), he did take steps to address the underlying causes of war, bringing about peace between traditional European enemies.

"I'm saving the best for last," Luis told me with a grin. "I always ended my morning strolls on the Île of Saint Louis at Berthillon's, an ice cream parlor. I thought it was fitting to have an ice cream shop there, as the island had been nothing but cow pastures back in the days of King Louis. It's on the Rue Saint-Louis, and has every flavor imaginable. I even had a cone of piña colada flavored gelato there! My favorite, if you can believe it, was a rose-flavored ice cream. You've got to go to Paris, if for nothing other than a taste of this delicacy!" Luis' eyes were sparkling from the taste memory.

Matanzas, Cuba
Wednesday, November 30, 2016 CE
9:00 a.m.

Fidel Castro died early on a Friday morning, November 25. Five days later the funeral procession was scheduled to pass through Matanzas as it headed east toward Santiago de Cuba, in a reversal of the 1959 Liberty Caravan that saw the Revolutionaries make their way west toward Havana. The ashes of the historic leader of Cuba's Revolution would be interred near the remains of Cuba's Apostle of Independence, José Martí. We weren't sure when the caravan would reach Matanzas, but it was supposed to be sometime before lunch. At around nine, I made the short one hundred and fifty-five step walk to the corner of Milanes and Santa Teresa at Liberty Park to take part in the vigil. Milanes Street was lined with people as far the eye could see.

When I reached the park, ready to pay my respects when the caravan passed, I heard my name called. Luis had spotted me, and motioned me to come and join him in the wait. He was standing in front of Triolet's, the Pharmacy Museum that serves as one of Matanzas' tourist destinations. The Museum is a replica of the nineteenth century working pharmacy that the French doctor Ernesto Triolet Lelievre founded and operated. Luis took advantage of our location to give me a thumbnail sketch of the pharmacy's place in Matanzas history, along with other examples of how the French had made their mark, such as the establishment of a French Quarter, now known as the barrio of Versalles. I learned about the architect Jules Sagebien, the visit of Jaques Cousteau and the *Calypso* to Matanzas Bay in search of sunken treasure, and other tidbits of French-Cuban trivia.

The subject changed when Luis asked me what I thought of the HBO movie that had just come out a few days before, *Mariela Castro's March: The LGBT Revolution in Cuba*. I told him I thought it was great, and I congratulated him, as he was one of the protagonists that Fidel's niece highlighted in the documentary. Luis, ever the cultural critic, responded that he wasn't crazy about it, that they left out a key part of his of his story. He proceeded to tell me the full story.

"First," he said, "there's the back story." He opened his wallet and pulled out a photo; it was of a young, twenty-something Luis. "Look at that photo," he said. "Look at those eyes, how they are sparkling." He explained to me that he had grown up in a loving family, and while he had known he was gay since he was a child, it was never an issue for his family. "I never had to come out of the closet, because I was never in a closet," he smiled as he obviously was recalling the love and affirmation he grew up with. When the Triumph of the Revolution occurred, he celebrated along with the rest of his friends; no one he knew supported the dictator Batista. So when the call to military service sounded, he and all his friends were ready to go, to do their part in defending the Revolution.

"This young man with the sparkling eyes was drafted at the age of twenty-four, and went to the assigned location. It was in the evening, and the Colonel in charge instructed us to board a bus. I thought I was going to my basic training camp. We rode all night on the bus, and arrived at our destination in Camagüey. What we found was not a training camp, it was a concentration camp, a forced labor camp. I would soon learn that I was in UMAP, the alternative to military service the government had set up for people with 'ideological deficiencies,' 'misfits,' those who didn't fit the standards of the 'New Man' of the Revolution. What was my deficiency? I was gay. They had rounded up gays, religious leaders, and vagrants and sent us all to UMAP to re-socialize us, sort of like the conversion therapy camps they have in the US. It was a year of horror. I had never experienced such aggression, such homophobia, such cruelty. They stole the light from my eyes. Remember the photo?"

Luis again showed me the bright, smiling face of his twenty-something photo. "Now, look at this," and Luis pulled a card out of his wallet. "This is the identity card they issued me when I left UMAP. Look at my face, my eyes; they are hollow, there's no life, no light." We stood there for a few minutes in silence, pondering the wounds that still ache from that year in the Camagüey camp.

"You know how I survived?" He asked. "There was a grace gift of beauty in the midst of that ugliness. It was there in UMAP that I fell in love for the first time. This is the part that HBO left out, the most important part of the story. I had a lover for the first time in my life, and we shared the terror together. It was intense, and lasted throughout the whole time we were in the camp. When we got out, we went our separate ways. My lover did what a lot of UMAP victims did, he left for the US. I couldn't do that. I couldn't leave my home. No matter what they had done to me, I was Cuban.

"That was the first time I struggled with the question of should I stay or should I go. I experienced the same struggle in the eighties when government officials tried to persuade me, along with many gay people, to get on the Mariel boats and leave Cuba. But the answer to the question was the same; there was no way I was going to abandon my land. Of course I would have loved to have had the chance to visit friends there and come back home, but the one chance I had at that, the US denied my visa."

As Luis finished his story, a hush fell over the waiting crowd. It was if they had all been listening to the saga, but no, there was news that the caravan was approaching. Everyone waited in reverent silence, and in a few minutes, here came the long line of military vehicles. They passed, and suddenly spontaneous shouts of *Yo soy Fidel* (I am Fidel) began filling the air. I looked at Luis, and he was weeping. I wondered what must be going through his mind, and asked him what he was feeling. He wiped his eyes and said solemnly, "Fidel Castro was our father. Like all fathers and sons, we had our problems, and he made his share of mistakes. But in the end, he was still our father, and in the end I am thankful for the Revolution; it has made a lot of important contributions in the world."

I couldn't help but ask him, "But Luis, after all you endured in UMAP, how could you continue supporting the Revolution?" He laughed and asked if I knew who Bola de Nieve was. I told him yes, he was the Cuban entertainer who reminded me of Louis Armstrong. He smiled. "A reporter asked Bola that same question one time. 'How is it possible that you, being homosexual, are revolutionary?' He answered: 'It must be because I like everything masculine, and this Revolution is very macho.'"

I laughed, and we stood there for a few more minutes, watching the crowd disperse, the cries of *Yo soy Fidel!* fading. Before parting ways, Luis offered one more reflection: "You know, you don't have to board a plane or a boat to travel the world. The world is always turning, always changing. What we saw today is another turning of the world. It won't be the same. With all the changes I have seen in my lifetime, I would consider myself a world traveler, even if I had never left Matanzas."

Epilogue

Walking with the Yuma[1]

Al final del viaje está el horizonte.
Al final del viaje partiremos de nuevo.
Al final del viaje comienza un camino,
otro buen camino que seguir descalzos, contando la arena.[2]

—SILVIO RODRÍGUEZ, AL FINAL DE ESTE VIAJE

Matanzas, Cuba
Saturday, October, 20, 2018 CE
3:00 p.m.

I got a new nickname today. For years, I have had the same generic street label as everyone from the US—*yuma,* the Cuban version of *gringo.* Oftentimes, I would be walking along the street and catch the world *yuma* emerging from a conversation on the opposite sidewalk, and my ears would perk up. I knew they were referencing me. At some point, I decided I would challenge their assumptions, and I began entering into those conversations,

1. "Yuma" is the Cuban label for foreigners, particularly foreigners from North America. More explanation to come later in the epilogue.

2. Translated: "At the end of the journey is the horizon. / At the end of the journey we part ways again. / At the end of the journey we begin a new path, / another good path that we follow barefoot, counting the sand." Rodríguez, Silvio. "Al final de este viaje en la vida." *Al final de este viaje.* Areito, 1978. Album.

108

using the best Cuban accent I could muster—*No me joda federaʹo, no soy yuma, soy matancero como tú.* "Don't mess with me, man, I'm not a *yuma*, I'm from Matanzas, like you." I enjoyed seeing the surprised facial expressions, and the occasional chuckle.

Today, someone invented my new nickname. I was meandering down Main Street, daydreaming, thinking about the significance of this holiday, Cuba's National Day of Culture, based on the date in 1868 when *the Bayamesa*, a song which came to be the National Anthem, was composed and first sung. I was trying to remember the lyrics, singing them in my mind: "To combat, run, Bayamesans! The homeland looks proudly upon you . . . la la la (*forgot the words*) . . . To live in chains is to be mired in shame and disgrace. Hear the sound of the bugle: To arms, brave ones, run!" I was thinking about how almost a century later, in the first year of my own life, this date would fall right in the middle of what came to be called the Crisis of October, or the Cuban Missile Crisis, as Fidel Castro's military was "running to arms," this time not with muskets but with Soviet nuclear weapons.

In the midst of my daydreaming, and the background noise of the city, that pesky word came into my hearing, and brought me back to reality. *Yuma.* I gave the same tried and true response I mentioned above, and along with the surprised expressions, someone in the group responded with a new word, *¡Sí, eres "yumatancero!"* "Yes, you are a 'yuma from Matanzas!'" The invented moniker would stick, and I soon began to hear people call out to me on subsequent walks down the city streets, *¡Hey! ¡yumatancero!* It never failed to bring laughter.

Matanzas, Cuba
Thursday, March 12, 2020 CE
8:00 a.m.

I open the door to our apartment and look across the patio to the open door of our neighbors' apartment. Orestes is making coffee, and Wanda comes out to water some plants. She sees me and offers her standard greeting, *¿Cómo está Están?* (How are you, Stan?) It's a running joke, a play on words, as people in Cuba have a hard time pronouncing my first name. There are no Spanish words that begin with the letters "st," so pronouncing that particular pair of letters requires a vowel at the beginning. So "Stan" became *Están.* Wanda came up with the joke years ago, to which I came up with a standard reply for her, *¿Cómo anda Wanda?* (How's it going, Wanda?)

The rest of our morning conversation revolves around the big news: the coronavirus has made it to Cuba and the government has announced its *quédateencasa* (stay at home) measures. We are only to go out for essentials (groceries). Other than those short ventures to the outside world, my daily "movement" in the foreseeable future will consist of descending the twelve steps to the second floor of the Kairos Center, walking the eleven steps around the balcony to the next staircase, descending another twelve steps (an appropriate number, as the church does house an AA Twelve-Step Program), to the ground floor. Once there, I take five steps over to the filtered-water faucets and fill up our gallon jugs for the day, and then make my daily two hundred and seventeen step journey around the building, checking out the sanctuary and office space, the kitchen and back patio, making sure no hooligans broke in during the night.

Throughout the day, I will make several of the ten-step journeys over to visit with or eat with Orestes and Wanda and their children. Some weeks later, Orestes and Wanda and Kim and I will begin getting more exercise, making weekly visits to the church members, dividing up the neighborhoods among us to check on everyone and deliver at-home worship resources.

Today, the day everything changed, seemed a good day to start writing my book. Kim and I had been scheduled to make a trip over the weekend to facilitate workshops and lead worship in a Fraternity of Baptist church in Bauta, a community in the Artemisa province not too far from Havana. Then, on Monday, we were scheduled to fly to North Carolina and spend a couple of weeks visiting family and friends. Our travel plans changed when the pastor in Bauta called to say that there was suspicion of a coronavirus case in the neighborhood (the first in the country), and they were having to cancel all the weekend activities. Like dominos (not the Cuban board game variety, but the tumbling effect variety), all plans were falling out of place. Kim and I did some quick investigating, and found that if we did board the plane on Monday, odds were we wouldn't be able to come back to Cuba anytime soon, as there would likely be travel bans in place.

We did some quick debating on the pros and cons of the Clash question: "Should I stay or should I go?" At the end of the debate, the scales tipped toward cancelling our flights, and we decided to stay. The anticipated travels bans would indeed be established for international travel, and on the local level bus and taxi services would be cancelled. Like many countries in the world, the citizenry (and temporary residents) of Cuba would soon be feeling the effects of cabin fever. And I would begin "feverishly" writing down stories that would evolve into this book.

While I would be writing out of a unique and fascinating context—experiencing firsthand how a very different culture and system from my own would deal with the threat of a pandemic, I never intended to write a book about coronavirus and COVID-19 in Cuba. Instead, in a general sense, I wanted to write a book about coming and going, about moving vs. staying in place, about the crazy-making effects of struggling with those competing impulses that have pulsed through human veins since Aganju and Yeyé Omo Eja made their first steps out of paradise. Being in semi-quarantine plays with our minds, largely because humanity is not 100 percent wired to stay at home. The nesting impulse is there, for sure, but it's only part of who we are. We also tend to go stir-crazy and feel the urge to fly the coop. Our internal homing beacon is balanced by the itch for adventure.

More particularly, I set out to write a book about how Cuba and Cubans put that conflict of competing voices in sharp relief. The sense of *patria*, homeland, is deeply woven in the *cubanía* DNA. But the *cubanía* itself, that sense of what defines Cuban culture, is not homegrown. It is a *jaiaca* (stew) comprised of cultures from all over the world, from people who left their original homelands—some by choice, some by force—to be part of the settling of the island. Indigenous, Spanish, African, French, Dutch, and many others—they are all part of the syncretistic stew, and have each contributed to the way Cubans talk, eat, sing, dance, worship and think. Now you can find the island's *cubanía* all over the world, as one pressure or another, one dream or another, has propelled some Cubans to decide to make the reverse journey back to the wider world from whence their ancestors came.

Lest we forget, the US also has a place in the long list of countries who have contributed to the Cuban identity. There has been a great diversity among the *yumas* who made their way here for one reason or another: US Vice-President William King came to recover from tuberculosis (he signed his oath of office in Matanzas), Dr. Henry Reeve to fight in the war for independence, Milton Hershey to process sugar for his kisses, Moses McCall to import Southern Baptist religion, Ernest Hemingway to go fishing and write Nobel Prize-winning stories, Meyer Lanksy to oversee mobster business, Barbara Dean to sing jazz, and Margaret Randall to hang out with bohemian poets, to name a few.

Then there was Willy Stokes and the Glory City crowd. Willy came over when he was still wearing diapers; his parents were among the two hundred US citizens on board the steamer *Yarmouth* that landed on the northern coast of the Camagüey province in January of 1900. They were part of a scheme of annexationists (people in the US who dreamed of colonizing Cuba and eventually converting it into the next state in the Union). Willy's parents and the others ventured to Cuba on blind faith, believing that a city called *La Gloria* awaited them.

The glory-bound travelers walked for days through swampy, mosquito-ridden forests and fields, until they finally arrived at the completely undeveloped plot of land they had bought (it turns out they had been conned by the Cuba Land and Steamship Company of New York). Some of them turned tail and went back; the ones who decided to stay built Glory City from scratch. Our friend Tulia, now priest of the Faithful to Jesus Episcopal Church in Matanzas, grew up there. Her grandmother had been an employee of Willy Stokes, helping take care of him and his house in the last years of his life. Willy was the last North American to live in *La Gloria*, before he departed for his eternal glory in 1974.

I suspect we all want to live in *La Gloria*, to revel in Glory, to build a glorious community, be it in the buggy Cuban swampland or the snaky Blue Ridge mountains. The rabbinic literature describes living in the sacred presence of God in terms of *shekinah*, a glorious God-infused space. Empires throughout world history have claimed to be manifestations of that divine level of glory, complete with messianic illusions of leadership and battle hymns for waging war against all other forms of community. *Glory, glory, hallelujah.* Many people doggedly defend their glory against attempted coups and conquests, while others abandon what they see as the faded glory of their fatherland and bolt off to find *La Gloria* in another shape and form. There are still others, fewer in number but important to the story, who see any attempt at establishing institutional glory as nothing more than a royal scam; for them the glorious life is the gypsy way, on the road, forever unfettered.

Jose Martí Airport, Havana, Cuba
December 20, 2020 CE
11:00 a.m.

I like to tell my Cuban friends that I was born and raised in the Land of the Sky[3]—it sounds good in Spanish, *la tierra del cielo*. It's where the horizon of the Blue Ridge mountains sometimes makes it hard to tell where earth stops and heaven starts. After going away to school and then spending a few years working in the North Carolina flatlands, I returned to the mountains in 1996, at age thirty-five, and made a home in Fairview, on land that has been in the family for five generations. *Fair view*. That's an appropriate description for my community, a place name that stands in humble contrast to the loftier "land of sky" moniker.

3. "Land of Sky" is a slogan applied to the mountains of western North Carolina.

Either way, whether in humility or pride, it was not hard to re-establish a root system back in the Blue Ridge hills, as my dad and uncle helped me and my wife, Kim, build a house within eyeshot of the stone chimney that is now the only thing remaining of my grandparents' old chestnut-board cabin. I imagined I would live there for the rest of my days, and often felt the truth of the poet James Still's lines: "I shall not leave these prisoning hills. . . I cannot leave. . . Being of these hills, I cannot pass beyond." To clarify: being imprisoned was not a bad thing, as the mountains enfolded me with a deep love of family, of culture, of heritage, of beauty. I was a willing captive. Then something happened. Cuba happened.

I made my first trip to the island in 1999, and experienced the allure of what I have come to call the "Cuba magic." With twenty-five trips over the next fifteen years, I began to understand the character of the magic; it has to do with contradictions. How is it that I experience such wealth (in spirit, in the arts, in education) in a society so relatively poor? How is it that I feel so much freer in a land lacking some of the basic civil liberties (free speech, free press) we take for granted in the states? How can a people presumably isolated from the world know so much more about what goes on around the globe than I do?

Through these excursions into Cuban life, the "prisoning hills" began to loosen their hold. So when a friend in Matanzas remarked one day in 2014, "You've been coming here for years on these one and two-week trips. When are you going to stay?" I heard it as a call, and it wasn't long before Kim and I were living in Matanzas, teaching at the ecumenical seminary there and working with the Fraternity of Baptist Churches of Cuba[4]

Six years later, I could have re-written James Still's poem to talk about how I could not imagine leaving "this prisoning island." I was captivated, again by love, for our Cuban family, the culture, the heritage, the beauty. Friends there might hear me use a typical Cuban phrase, or see me at a neighbor's door drinking a five-cent espresso, or hear me playing a Silvio Rodríguez song on the guitar, and exclaim, *¡Eres 100% Cubano!* "You are 100 percent Cuban!" or, *¡Eres más Cubano que nosotros!* "You are more Cuban than we are!" While I know good and well it is not true, I always appreciate their blessing, and am happy to be on my way toward making the affirmations real.

And now, December 20, 2020, we find ourselves on our way back to Fairview. We had to leave. A confluence of pandemic, increasing material

4. The Fraternity of Baptist Churches in Cuba is the denomination with whom we work. It is a partner denomination to the Alliance of Baptists in the US, both having been founded in the late 1980s in response to the growing fundamentalism in their respective Baptist conventions.

scarcities, and political unrest led the Cuban government to cease issuing the year-long temporary residence visas like the one we had been working under, so we headed back to the hills. Here we are, with a "fair view" of mountain grandeur, knowing that this is still home to us. We do belong here, but we also find ourselves longing for our other home beyond the land of the sky's horizon. I suspect if we live long enough, we will make the pilgrimage back and forth between these two captivating landscapes many times, and will always feel the tension between longing and belonging.

Charlotte, N.C.
Friday, September 24, 2021 CE
7:30 a.m.

I, *eStán*, the *yumatancero* exiled back to his original homeland of the Blue Ridge when COVID began raging in Cuba, find myself today sitting in the Charlotte Airport, getting ready for a thirty-six hour ordeal of a flight itinerary that will eventually land me in Havana for five days of quarantine, followed by three weeks of renewed friendship in Matanzas. I have four copies of the draft of this book, translated into Spanish, ready to share with my protagonists (ah, if only Luis were still around, to read his draft). This flight, the first one I could find after months of searching, has the quality of a good country music song, "It took me 9,000 miles to get to your door, 90 miles away." For I'll be flying from Charlotte to New York, New York to Madrid, and Madrid to Havana. *A-ah-ahh-ah, ah-ah-ahh-ah!*

I think about how unique each of these places is. Matanzas is distinct from Havana. Havana is different from Madrid. Madrid is a poles apart from New York. New York is another world from Charlotte. And Charlotte is a stark contrast to where the journey started, in my Fairview home in the Blue Ridge Mountains, the Land of the Sky.

I realize as I write this that "Land of the Sky" sounds like an expansive space. To be honest, though, during my growing up years of the late 1960s and early 1970s the world I knew was anything but expansive; it was tightly contained within the small range of mountains that encircled my home in the valley. I knew little of what existed outside that circle of hills. For instance, I'm sure I could not have placed Cuba on a map if my childhood life depended on it, nor could I have picked Fidel Castro out of a lineup. For all I knew, the Bay of Pigs was a barbecue joint at the beach. And even though my Uncle Don had been on a Marine ship patrolling the Cuban waters during the crisis of October, I never heard a word about it.

The one thing I do remember hearing about Cuba in my childhood was the oft-repeated news reports of planes that had been hijacked to Havana. The idea that one could plan a vacation or business trip and board a plane, only to have the destination altered by armed passengers, fascinated me, and frightened me. My first experience of flying would not come until years later, when I was in my twenties, but even then, as I boarded the plane in Asheville headed for New York, I looked around to see if I could spot potential hijackers. Where might they take me?

As I entered my forties, the trajectory of my life was pretty well settled. You might say it was fixed, pre-determined by the five or six generations of mountaineers for whom the question "should I stay or should I go" had a consistent answer: *stay*. And when there was a need to *go*, such as the call to war, it was clear that the goal was to come back, hopefully all in one piece. There was never any talk of the earlier generations who had answered the question differently, who had pulled up roots in Ireland and Scotland and Germany to cross the ocean to a new world. I do not know their stories. My own journey of life, up until that fourth decade, was confined to the small steps of family, work, and church that moved me in and around the Blue Ridge Mountain chain.

Were the news reporters to describe what happened to me at the turn of the millennium, they might well describe it as a hijacking. The preacher in me would call it a holy hijacking. The Spirit took control of the cockpit and announced a different destination. Twenty years later, I, the mountaineer *yuma*, would feel as rooted in Matanzas as I had in Fairview. Dozens of short-term trips had led to several years of full-time work, and once again, it seemed that my trajectory was set. The work was fulfilling, the culture was fascinating, and the people were loving and welcoming.

And then there was another hijacking, a course reversal. As COVID took hold and the Cuban economy began to suffocate from the increased strangulation of the US embargo, the social fabric began to unravel, and the Cuban government decided not to renew any long-term visas. A group of good friends from the Fraternity of Baptists, who were responsible for our visa process, called us to a meeting in early December and broke the news; we couldn't stay. So we boarded a plane in late December, 2020, and found ourselves once again gazing at the outline of the surrounding mountains in the Land of the Sky.

Nine months later, as I sit in the airport, I am reminded of a book I read many years ago, *I Am One of You Forever*, by the western North Carolina author Fred Chappell. The title describes his feelings of connection to the mountain people. I resonated deeply with the book, and still do, but now I understand there is a larger set of *You* of which I am a part. For sure, our large circle of US family and friends will forever be part of the *you* of which I am one, but now they are joined by Sila and Orestes and Alexis and Lázaro and Luis and so many others of our Cuban circle. I suspect the holy hijackings will continue, with trips back and forth, until we find a way to be "settled" while in constant motion. The world keeps turning, so like it or not, there will be many more journeys, many more walks. At the end of one journey is the horizon of another. No doubt there will be many more stories to tell, more words to desccribe the everyday comings and goings of a beautiful and resilient people. Who knows where the stories will lead us?

¿A dónde van las palabras. . .?
¿Acaso flotan eternas. . .?
¿A dónde van?[5]

THE END

5. Translated: "Where do the words go. . .? Do they float on forever. . .? Where are they going?" Rodríguez, Silvio, "¿A Dónde Van?" *Mujeres*. Fonomusic, 1978. Album.